Amy Bloom is the author of the nov
collections of prize-winning stories: *Come to Me* and *A Blind Man Can See How Much I Love You*. She teaches Creative Writing at Yale University, where she is a fellow of Calhoun College.

re praise for *Where the God of Love Hangs Out*:

'*Where the God of Love Hangs Out* is brilliant. The stories are shocking and lovely' Roddy Doyle, *Guardian*

ully astute . . . The subtle, stirring title story ably illustrates Ms. Bloom's remendous gift for imagining life as a series of choices, with the paths not ken as vivid as the ones that are' *New York Times*

characters are never less than sympathetically rendered, making it hard ve them behind' *Vogue*

e of the most sublime brief fictions currently being published . . . a pitch t collection' *Herald*

er sentences are clear and inviting, her plots have arcs, and moment by moment the stories ring emotionally true. This is unrelentingly pleasurable fiction . . . Bloom's writing manages to be at once light and grave. She takes her characters with a seriousness that makes them real. That is the odd, neat trick of all good fiction' Lionel Shriver, *Financial Times*

'Amy Bloom has the gift of drawing you into her fictional worlds so swiftly and acquainting you with her characters so deftly that, within a few short sentences, you feel you must have known these people and places in a previous life . . . Bloom shows us love in all its glorious, painful complexity' *Jewish Chronicle*

'These sensitive stories each capture moments at which body or heart are at breaking point . . . The finely wrought sentences are short and taut, as if the often incapacitated characters are wasting no time in telling their tales . . . In Bloom's capable hands, the short story is perfect for depicting lives in which love hangs out in snatched, secret moments of hectic days' *Observer*

'She writes in beautifully wrought prose, with spunky humour and a flair for delectably eccentric details. Her narrative talents include a fine touch with flashbacks, which she handles as suavely as any writer I can think of. Her gift for dialogue is equally terrific . . . Brava, Ms Bloom. Send us an equally sly, dashing book very soon, please' *Scotsman*

'Her characters are very believable, of the moment, and also original and surprising. Above all, her writing is lovely: the words sparkle along, in the speedy river of wit which is almost a hallmark of the contemporary American short story. It's a highly entertaining style, and the juxtaposition of that wisecracking Woody Allen-ish voice with profound insights into the human heart is highly effective . . . This is a great piece of fiction, thought provoking, and highly entertaining' Éilís Ní Dhuibhne, *Irish Times*

'Amy Bloom is a fine writer, really a very fine writer: a scrupulous observer of widely varying human types and the precise kinds of bric-a-brac they surround themselves with, a maker of exceedingly elegant sentences, and a sophisticated storyteller' James Lasdun, *Guardian*

'For a collection that promises such a grand revelation in its title, it is beautifully understated. Love is not a victory march, as Leonard Cohen famously wrote; for Bloom, it is a series of tiny incidents, actions, even silences that crystallise over time into that rare human emotion' *Independent on Sunday*

'Bloom describes love affairs with great humanity and in tender sensual terms . . . The warmth and compassion of her fiction owe much to her gift for conveying the humour of intimate transactions without belittling them' *Times Literary Supplement*

'Amy Bloom's short stories and her novels portray human relationships with an insight that can leave the reader feeling as rattled as they are compelled; her fiction sees so much, so piercingly that, reading Bloom's sentences, you begin to wonder if you have been walking around with your eyes fully open at all . . . *Where the God of Love Hangs Out* throws an unforgettable floodlight on to unforgettable corners of experience . . . situations particular to her complicated characters reach the reader with uncanny – almost uncomfortable – intimacy thanks to the richness and penetration of Bloom's writing' Belinda McKeon, *Irish Times*

Where the God of Love Hangs Out

Amy Bloom

GRANTA

Granta Publications, 12 Addison Avenue, London W11 4QR

First published in Great Britain by Granta Books 2010
This paperback edition published by Granta Books 2011

Some of the stories in this work originally appeared in the following: "Compassion and Mercy" in *Granta,* Summer, 2009; "By-And-By" in *Ms.,* Summer, 2004; "Between Here and Here" in *Narrative,* December, 2009; "Your Borders, Your Rivers, Your Tiny Villages" in *Ploughshares,* Fall, 2002; "The Old Impossible" in *Ploughshares,* Fall, 2006; "I Love to See You Coming, I Hate to See You Go" in *Tin House,* Spring, 2004; and "Permafrost" in *Yale Review,* January, 2010.

Grateful acknowledgment is made to the following for permission to reprint previously published material:

HarperCollins Publishers and Pan Macmillan, London: "Sleepwalking" from *Come to Me* by Amy Bloom, copyright © 1993 by Amy Bloom. Rights in the United Kingdom are controlled by Pan Macmillan, London. Reprinted by permission of HarperCollins Publishers and Pan Macmillan, London.

Jane Hirshfield: "When Your Life Looks Back" and "Opening the Hands Between Here and Here" by Jane Hirshfield, copyright © 2008 by Jane Hirshfield. All rights reserved. Reprinted by permission of the author.

Random House, Inc., and Pan Macmillan, London: "Night Vision" and "Light into Dark" from *A Blind Man Can See How Much I Love You* by Amy Bloom, copyright © 2000 by Amy Bloom. Rights in the United Kingdom are controlled by Pan Macmillan, London. Reprinted by permission of Random House, Inc.

A CIP catalogue record for this book is available from the British Library.

1 3 5 7 9 10 8 6 4 2

ISBN 978 1 84708 169 8

Book design by Susan Turner

Printed and bound in Great Britain
by CPI Bookmarque, Croydon

For Brian

CONTENTS

WHERE THE GOD OF LOVE HANGS OUT

YOUR BORDERS, YOUR RIVERS, YOUR TINY VILLAGES

At two o'clock in the morning, no one is to blame.

We'd been watching CNN, one scene of disaster leading to the next, the reporter in front of what might have been a new anthrax outbreak giving way to the military analyst in the studio with new developments in Kabul, when William put his hand on my breast. My husband was asleep upstairs, dreaming of making the deal that would put us on high ground when the entire economy collapsed, and William's wife was asleep in the guest room, getting her restorative eight hours. I think of Isabel as forcefully regular and elegant in all of her habits, and I'm sure she thinks of me as a little askew in all of mine.

William's hand trembled slightly. Our two plain gold wedding bands twinkled in the light of the TV screen. He touched my breast through my bathrobe and my pajamas—I had dressed for watching TV with William as if for bundling—for a very long time. His touch, left forefinger on left nipple, through wool and flannel, should have been numbing in its dreamy repetition, but it was not; it captured my whole body's attention. We kept our eyes on the TV. Finally, he fumbled under my robe and opened two buttons of my pajama top. His hand moved across my breast, and I sighed. I heard him breathing, hard and damp, and I put my hand on his big belly. It does not seem possible that we are people with three children, two marriages, and a hundred and ten years between us.

The first time I made out in a car, it was with Roger Saleta from Far Rockaway. We were trying to end the war in Vietnam by flooding the local draft board with mail and marching in front of it whenever our class schedules allowed. I had spoken at a big rally, wearing an electric-blue nylon halter top and my tight bell-bottoms with a crucified Jesus painted on the right leg. (I pretended not to know, and it may have been that I actually did not know then, why some people found this offensive. "I'm not mocking Jesus," I told my mother. "I'm just representing him, on my jeans.") Roger circled around the parking lot after the rally and offered me a ride in his gold Camaro. We drove to Jones Beach, miles from the protest, miles from social studies and home ec, and we stayed in the car while the waves crashed and we worked at each other. Hands and mouths. Necks and elbows. He licked me through my jeans until they were wet and dark blue from inseam to belt buckle. I wanted to bang my head against the back of the seat from pleasure, and dug my hands into his black curls instead. This boy, not my idea of a lover, not even my idea of a date, had my body humming, dancing its tiny, fierce dance in the backseat. His hands under me and his mouth shamelessly pressed against me, as if the rest of the world could sink into the ocean out there and we would not even blink, or maybe, yes, blink dully, just once, before we returned to the real world of my pussy and his mouth. Later, we went to his prom, and I saw that he couldn't dance, which I hadn't known, and that his eyes were much too close together, which I had known and ignored, and I was a big disappointment to him that night.

* * *

William whispered something to me, but they were showing night bombing in the north and I couldn't hear him over the shouting correspondent. "May I?" he said again, and put his mouth over my nipple. William is English, and he has beautiful manners. He has never failed to open the door, to pull out the chair, to slip off the coat, to bring flowers and send thank-you notes. It is not an affectation. Charles, my husband, is the same way, and it's not an affectation in him, either. They are both sons of determined English mothers and quiet American fathers who let their wives have their way. Charles and William are friends, Isabel and I are friends. It is all just as bad as it sounds. The close friendship has always been between me and William, from the moment we stood snickering together at that first faculty meeting until now. Everybody knows that William and I are, inexplicably but truly, best friends. I think his size and my shyness, and, of course, Isabel's beauty and Charles's good looks, gave us permission to love each other and hold hands in public, looking, I'm sure, like a woolly mammoth and a stiff-tailed duck, just that odd and just that ridiculous.

Even when they moved back to Boston after their one year in New Haven, back to his university and her real estate, we stayed friends. Isabel and I have had pedicures together, we've dissected our husbands and considered the possibility that a little collagen around the mouth might not be a bad idea. All four of us have sat at our kitchen tables, talking through their daughter's suicidally bad time in Prague and our son Danny's near-engagement to an awful girl from Bryn Mawr. I like that William is such a good storyteller; she likes that Charles is so clever with his hands. When we visit, she gives him a "Honey Do" list and he pops around their house with his toolbox all afternoon and Isabel follows behind, handing him nails and a caulk gun, while William and I play Scrabble. She used to asked me for advice on getting William to watch his weight, which I gave, which was useless, and I felt terrible for her. After his first heart attack, she called me in tears, and I thought, Well, of course he has got to exercise and drink less and stop smoking and cut out the bacon and if I were his wife I would have him on egg whites and a thimbleful of sherry, but I'm not. William called me from the hospital and said, "Please eat some butter for me." We continued to meet at every intriguing restaurant he'd hear about, Abbott's Lobster in the Rough, Ma Glockner's for the chicken dinner, and we spent half a day finding a little place in Kent that had outstanding macaroni and cheese.

We've come to our quartet already grown up, with our long-standing convictions and habits and odd ways in place, and none of us has changed very much since we met. Isabel is much fitter and William is a little fatter and Charles dropped tennis for golf, coming home flushed and handsome, cursing cheerfully about his handicap and his stroke. Charles and William and Isabel e-mail one another news every day, and when we're together, Charles and William watch CNN for hours, drinking their Guinness. They talk like they've just come from a meeting with the Joint Chiefs of Staff, and Isabel joins in, perching on the end of the sofa near William, clucking her tongue when the scroll at the bottom of the screen says: AIR STRIKES HIT ALL AL QAEDA TRAINING CAMPS IN AFGHANISTAN . . . DURING THE RAID ON BEIT JALA, ISRAELI FORCES ARRESTED 10 PALESTINIANS AND KILLED 6. I don't know if she is clucking because six isn't enough or because it is way too much. Isabel reads *The Wall Street Journal* and *The New York Times* every day and I don't. It's not as if I waltz around the homestead with a big bow in my blond curls, picking daisies and waiting for the grown-ups to sit down to the nice dinner I've made. I teach, I go to the movies, I talk to my grown sons frequently (Adam is a news-watcher, Danny is a news-avoider, and all that matters to me is that they both live in small, safe towns in the Midwest and neither has children). I don't watch the news with my friends' avidity; I have not constructed a mental map of Afghanistan so that I can track troops, bombs, and food drops, and I will not even discuss whether or not we should call Bobby Bernstein, Charles's new golfing partner, and ask him for doxycycline.

William and I had a date to watch *Mrs. Dalloway.* Charles and Isabel had kissed good night, the way we often kiss one another, something more than lips on cheek, nicely suggestive of restrained passion, as if, under the right circumstances, Charles and Isabel and William and I would just fall upon each other.

"Let's watch a bit of the news first," William said. I made popcorn for later. We would sit with my feet in his lap, and he would ask for another beer and more salt, and I would get it. Then William would sigh with pleasure at having everything he wanted, and so would I.

The Appalachian Trail through New Jersey is like the road to hell. My boyfriend Danny and I slogged through swamp and low water, past dozens of orange blazes, which indicated not trail but possible paths through purgatory, until in the dark we found a flat, meadowy place. As soon as we stopped moving, mosquitoes descended upon us, attacking every moist, warm spot. They flew into our eyes, our mouths, our ears, burrowing through our wet, salty hair to our scalps. Trying to be quick in their buzzing black fog, we threw down our tarps and our sleeping bags and dove into them, clothes and boots still on. It was eighty degrees outside and perhaps ninety-five in our sleeping bags, but the choice was to be bitten all night or lie in pools of sweat until dawn. Danny zipped our bags together, and we rolled back to back, rank and itching and, as I recall, furious with each other—me because he had picked the trail into Rattlesnake Swamp, him because I laughed unkindly every time he unfolded our Sierra Club map that afternoon and said, "This looks right." Just before dawn, the bugs disappeared to digest and rest up to prepare for the second wave. Danny, the gentlest of boys, willowy and devoted, slid on top of me, rolled my underpants down to my ankles with one hand, pushed my legs apart, and came into me like a stranger. We lay there, stuck together from hip to collarbone, faces turned away, until it was light enough to leave.

William said, "Come here, on top of me. Come sit on my lap, darling." In six years, he has never called me anything but my name. Just one time, when we were chatting on the phone and his other line rang, he said, "Hold on a tick, dear." I climbed up on him, just as he asked, and draped myself over his stomach, resting my face against his shoulder, kissing it through his shirt. I unbuttoned his collar and ran my fingers around his thick neck, into his hair and down through the gray hairs beneath his undershirt.

"Oh, yes," he said. I turned around and lay back against him, and he cupped my breasts under my pajama top, and we watched Jeff Greenfield and then the young woman who dyed her hair brown to go to Afghanistan. "At least it's not Fox," William said. "Fox News, bloody Bill O'Reilly. Pandering little hairball." He put his hands around my waist and pressed me close to him, and I could feel his stomach, his shirt buttons, his belt buckle against my spine, and his very hard erection underneath me.

I said I could feel him, and I put my head back so he would kiss my neck. He slid his lips up and down, and then his teeth and then his tongue. He pressed me closer. "You should have known me twenty years ago," he said. "Thirty years ago. Back in my flowering youth." I said that I was just as glad not to have known him in his flowering youth and that it had never occurred to me that I would know him this way, even in his autumnal splendor.

"What now?" he said, and we both looked to the right and the left, to Isabel on one side and Charles on the other and the television in front of us. I shrugged and I felt William shrug, too. "Face me," he said. "I miss seeing you, otherwise."

I swung around and unbuttoned another button. "This is so terrible," I said, and I think he wasn't sure if I meant what we were watching or what we were doing.

"We are not terrible people," he said.

He was so big, there was so much to him; it was a great comfort, to find warm flesh everywhere I turned, his big thighs beneath me, like ground. At the beach last summer, he'd kept to his linen pants and guayabera ("Fat men may not appear in bathing suits," he said), but he showed his broad white feet, in the sand. I thought every part of him must be a pink-tinged white, wide and thick and immaculately kept. His heart was beating like a drum.

"This could be it," he said. "The big bang. That would take some explaining."

"It won't be your problem," I said, and he laughed, bouncing me in his lap a little.

"Touch me," he said.

I unzipped his pants and reached into his big blue-striped shorts and held his penis in my hand. I touched him as best I could, moving my fingers in the small space beneath his belly, in the little cave of his pants and boxers. He put his head back and closed his eyes, and he looked just the way he did at our lunches, greedy and delighted and deeply attentive. His whole body shuddered when he came, and even before his eyes were open, he'd pulled out a beautiful white handkerchief and cleaned up.

"Messy," he said. "Marvelous." He cleared his throat and put the handkerchief away. "Darling. Something for you?" He picked me up and laid me back on the couch. I shook my head. I still had my socks and slippers and everything else on. William took my slippers off.

"What a little chatterbox you are," he said, and while I was laughing, he knelt down on the floor in front of me, muttering about his knees and the state of our carpeting, and pulled my pajama bottoms down and put his face between my legs. I put his glasses next to mine on the coffee table. When he got back up on the couch, breathing like a freight train and smoothing out my pajamas, Greta Van Susteren was still answering questions on her show, which William said was an excellent forum for the slightly informed. He handed me the remote.

"Turn it off, please," he said. "Put your head here."

I laid my head on his shoulder again and put my slippers back on.

"It's almost three," I said.

"I know," he said. "Not yet."

We held hands, and then he hoisted himself up, bringing me with him.

"People," he said. I nodded.

"No harm done, I hope? You're not going to look at me tomorrow with barely disguised horror?"

"No," I said. "Nothing like that."

I put away the popcorn and rinsed the bowl while William finished his beer.

"How about a cigar?" he said.

William has moved to cigars from cigarettes, not exactly the dramatic change his doctors hoped for, and moved from cream in his coffee to fat-free half-and-half, which he now talks about the way other men talk about working out. When he smokes, I take a few puffs, to be companionable.

We sat on the back porch, the wood cold under my ass. "Do you need a coat?" he asked.

"I'm fine. How about you? You don't have a jacket on."

"I keep me warm," he said. "My thermostat is set rather high." The moon shone through the clouds.

"The leaves are going," he said.

I puffed on his cigar.

"William," I said.

He stood up slowly, using the banister for leverage.

"It's still a beautiful night," he said. He lay down on the ground. "Climb on," he said. "Let's go for a ride."

The moon lit up the whole yard and William, white beneath me. I folded my robe and tucked it under his head. Tiny leaves shook loose, bronze snow floating down upon us, sticking gently in my hair and his, until we were almost covered.

I LOVE TO SEE YOU COMING, I HATE TO SEE YOU GO

William has gout.

It is the worst and most embarrassing pain of his life. His true nature, his desires and hidden history are revealed. By his foot.

Before he can get to the phone, the machine picks up.

"It's me. I heard the gout's back. Call me."

Clare's messages are always like this, concerned and crabby, as if having to make the call will cause her—probably has caused her; the plane is pulling away even as she speaks—to miss her flight.

"I'm here," William says.

"Okay, do you want to just get Thai in Springfield?"

Springfield is almost halfway between Clare's house and his. William doesn't have the energy even for Thai in Springfield.

"Christ. Why don't you just drive up here and bring lunch?" He would like to patch things up with Clare, but just putting down the phone drives two long, thick needles of uric acid deep into his ankle. He should have flowers in the house. He should shave. It won't be romantic.

Clare gets her car washed and drives up. She has to make sure that her visit takes place when her husband won't want to come, and there are things she cannot cancel and things she doesn't want to cancel, and in the end she sticks a note on her door, changing her office hours, and loads up the car. Usually she brings William corned beef on rye, or pâté and pumpernickel, and a big can of Guinness, and once, when they were right in the thick of things, she brought a box of Krispy Kremes and a bottle of Sancerre, but none of that is right for someone with gout. She packs two cooked, skinless chicken breasts, blanched broccoli, a basket of Maine blueberries (she read up after the first attack, and every Web site said blueberries), a box of chocolate soy shake, and a little tub of tofu. It's not romantic.

Clare knocks twice and comes in. If Isabel were there, they'd hug and kiss before she was ushered into the Presence. And if Isabel were upstairs and not too close by, William would kiss Clare hard on the lips and then he'd ask her to do things that he wouldn't ask of Isabel. If Isabel were there, she'd make Clare stay over when it got late, and lend her her own ivory linen pajamas. Clare would lie awake listening for William and imagining him listening for her, under the faded pink comforter, in his daughter's old room. Neither one of them would slip down the hall at two A.M., they wouldn't expect it of each other, but at breakfast, while Isabel showered, Clare would look at William with a sort of friendly disdain, and he would look at her as if she were selling drugs to schoolchildren.

William calls her name from the living room. He would get up, but it hurts too much. He usually shaves twice a day. He usually wears custom-made shirts and mossy, old-fashioned cologne, and he would prefer not to have Clare see him in backless bedroom slippers and green baggy pants, dragging his foot from room to room like road kill, but when he says so, she laughs.

"I've seen you worse," she says, and there is no arguing with that. It seems to William that Clare last saw him looking good, well dressed and in control of himself a year and a half ago, before they were lovers. Now she's seen him riddled with tubes, hung left and right with plastic pouches, sweating like a pig through a thin hospital gown that covered about a third of him.

Clare puts her groceries away in Isabel's kitchen. Isabel has been telling William to change his ways for twenty years, and now he has to. Clare puts the chicken breasts in the refrigerator and thinks that that must be nice for Isabel.

William sits back in his armchair, moving his right foot out of harm's way. If Clare gently presses his foot or lets the cuff of her pants just brush against his ankle, it will hurt worse than either of his heart attacks. He sees Clare angling toward him and moves his leg back a little more.

"Don't bump me," he says.

"I wasn't *going* to bump you."

Clare sits on the arm of the chair and glances at his foot. It's her job not to take any notice of it. She can notice the slippers and green gardening pants, and she can say something clever about it all, if she can think of something clever, which she can't. Isabel says clever, kind things to William when he's under the weather. Clare's seen it. Isabel arranges him beautifully, she flatters him into good behavior, she buys chairs that fit him and finds huge, handsome abstracts to balance the chairs; she drapes herself around him like wisteria and she carries his hypertension pills, his indomethacin, his cholesterol pills, and his prednisone in an engraved silver case, as if it's a pleasure. The last time William and Clare had sex, William rested above Clare, just for a minute, catching his breath. He slipped off his elbows, and his full weight fell onto her. "Jesus Christ," she'd said. "You could kill someone." William did laugh but it's not something she likes to remember.

"God, it's like a giant turnip," Clare says, putting her hand over her mouth.

It is exactly like a giant turnip and William is happy to hear her say so. His heart rises on a small, breaking wave of love just because

Clare, who says the precisely wrong and tactless thing as naturally as breathing, is with him, and will be right here for almost twenty-four hours.

"Really, cooked turnip."

"Well, the skin begins peeling in a couple of days, the doctor says, so it'll be even more disgusting. Hot, peeling, naked turnip." He leans forward and kisses the shoulder closer to him.

"Did Isabel leave food for you?"

"Hardly any. The three things I can eat. When she comes back the two of you can have a big party, tossing back shots of vodka, licking caviar out of the jar."

"Isabel wouldn't do that to you."

"You would."

"Probably," Clare says, and bends to kiss him. Everything she thought about while driving up, how much trouble he is and how selfish and where all that shameless piggery has gotten him (gout and her), is nothing when he kisses her, although even when their lips touch, even as the soft, salty tip of his tongue connects to hers, they are not the best kisses she's ever had.

When they stop kissing, William says, "Take off that ugly brown coat and stay a while, won't you?"

A month before the gout attack, Clare made William come with her to visit her uncle David. William clutched the staircase with both hands and made her carry his hat, his jacket, and the bottle of wine.

"You didn't say it was a walk-up."

"It's two flights, William, that's all. Just rest for a minute."

It was a bad idea. William said it, panting up the stairs, and he said it again when Uncle David went into his kitchen to get William a glass of water. Uncle David said it when William went to use the bathroom.

William washed his face with cold water and took his hypertension pills. He looked at the Viagra pills he'd been carrying around, in a tiny square of plastic wrap twisted like the wax-paper salt shakers his mother made for picnics. He'd been hoping for several weeks that he and Clare would go for a very elegant autumnal picnic in the Berkshires and that afterward they would stop into one of the seedy motels on Route 183. (When they did finally have the picnic and they did find the Glen Aire motel, the Viagra mixed badly with William's hypertension pills, and right after getting the kind of erection the online pharmacy had promised, he passed out. Clare drove them home in her aggressive, absent-minded way, blasting the horn and sprinkling the remaining six blue pills out the window, as William rested, his face against the glass.)

"What do I want to meet him for?" Uncle David said. "He seems like a nice man but I like Charles."

"He's my best friend. That's all. I wanted my best friend to meet my favorite relative."

"Only relative." David shrugged.

It was so clearly a bad idea, and so clearly understood by all parties to be a bad idea, that Clare thought she should just take William back downstairs and send her uncle a box of chocolates and a note of apology.

William came out of the bathroom, mopping his face, and shook Clare's uncle's hand again.

"Nice place. I'm sorry Clare made me come."

"Me, too. She's hard to argue with."

The two men smiled, and William picked up his coat.

"Those stairs'll kill you," David said. "Why don't you have a beer, and then go."

They had their beers as if Clare wasn't there. They talked about baseball, as the season was under way, and they talked about electric cars, which was even more boring than baseball. Clare sat on the windowsill and swung her feet.

William used the bathroom again before they left. David and Clare looked at each other.

David said, "You can't hide someone that big. Where would you put him, sweetheart? He'd stick out of the closet and you can't put a man like that under the bed."

Clare knew Charles was never going to walk in on her and William. It was probably not a great idea to sleep with William; she knew it wasn't a great idea almost immediately after it happened. She had managed to upend something that had sat neatly and foursquare beneath them, and even if William shouldered the blame, even if Charles was good enough to blame William, Clare never thought you could fault a man for taking sex when it was offered, any more than you'd blame the dog for flinging himself on a scrap that missed the plate. She knew she'd done more than just tilt the friendship between the four of them, but she was not ruining their lives with brilliantined paramours, sidecars, and cuckolds, the way her uncle made it sound. She was not ruining their lives at all, and you might think that the man known in her family as the Lord Byron of Greater Nyack would understand that.

"What can I say?"

"He makes you feel so young?" David sang. "He makes you feel like spring has sprung, songs must be sung? Like that?"

"No. You don't have to be ugly about it. I think . . . I make him feel alive."

David shook his head. "I'm sure you do. That's what these things are for."

Clare looked out the living room window and counted three women pushing strollers, four boys smoking cigarettes, seven bags of garbage.

"Don't bring him again."

"I get it," Clare said. "I'm sorry."

"You're not listening to me. Don't do this."

"All *right.*"

William walked in to see Uncle David whispering in Clare's ear and Clare pulling on her coat. William would rather have danced naked in a Greyhound bus station, he would rather have danced naked wearing a big pink party hat and matching pink boots, than stay another minute in Clare's uncle's apartment.

The men shook hands again and Clare kissed her uncle on the cheek, and he patted her face. They didn't like to fight.

In the car William said, "What was that for?"

"I thought you'd like each other."

"You embarrassed him," William said, and he thought it was just like her to make that perfectly decent old man meet her lover and force him—not that she ever thought she forced anything upon anyone—to betray Charles by saying nothing or to betray Clare, which of course he would never do. It was just exactly like Clare to act as if it'd been a pleasant visit under normal circumstances.

William dropped Clare off at the university parking lot and drove back to Boston. She watched him pull away, the gray roof silver from the halogen street lamps, the inside brightened for just a second by the green face of his phone and the deep yellow flare of his lighter.

At four o'clock, William takes the round of pills Isabel left in a shot glass by the kitchen sink. At five, he falls asleep, and Clare reads their newspaper and then William's old *Economists*. At six, while William snores in his recliner, she calls Charles to say that William is under the weather, Isabel is still on duty with her mother, and she, Clare, will stay overnight with William. As she talks, Clare gets her sweater out of the dining room and kicks her shoes into the rattan basket in the front hall.

"Don't kill him," Charles says. Clare is not famous for her bedside manner.

"He's a pain in the ass," Clare says, and it's not just her faint reflexive wish to throw Charles, and everyone, off the track. Isabel and Charles and all of their combined children could walk through the house right now, looking for trouble, and there'd be no sign, no scent, no stray, mysterious thread, of anything except an old, buckling friendship.

William snorts and wakes up, his hair wild and waving like silver palm fronds. He looks like he might have had a bad dream, and Clare smiles to comfort him. He looks at her as if he's never seen her, or never seen her like this, which isn't so; he's seen her a hundred times just like this, seated across from him deep in thought, flinging her legs over the arm of the chair to get comfortable.

"Oh, here you are," he says.

Clare drops the magazine on the floor. William looks encouragingly at the handsome bamboo magazine rack on the other side of the chair, and Clare stands up.

"Do you want some dinner?"

"How can you?" William asks. "What kind of dinner?"

"Aren't you the most pathetic thing." Clare walks over to smooth his dream-blown hair. They stay like this so long, her hands on his head, his head against her chest, that neither one of them can think of what the next natural thing to do is.

"We could go to bed," William says.

Clare goes into the kitchen, gathers up everything that wasn't eaten at lunch and every promising plastic container, including a little olive tapenade and a lot of pineapple cottage cheese, and lays it all on the coffee table in front of William with a couple of forks and two napkins.

"You do go all out," he says.

"I don't know how Isabel caters to you the way she does. If Charles were as much of a baby as you, I'd get a nurse and check into a hotel."

"I'm sure you would."

He doesn't say again that they could go to bed; she heard him the first time. That lousy picnic might have been the last time. This might not be the farewell dinner (and you could hardly call it dinner—it's not even a snack, it's what a desperately hungry person with no taste buds might grab while running through a burning house), but it has that feeling. She's brought him sensible food, and no wine; she hasn't made fun of his slippers or the gardening pants; she's worn her ugly brown coat and not the pretty blue one they bought together in Boston. An intelligent, disinterested observer would have to say it doesn't look good for the fat man.

"Let's go to bed," Clare says. Husbands and wives can skip sex, without fuss, without it even being a cause for fuss, but Clare can't imagine how you say to the person whom you have come to see for the express purpose of having sex, Let's just read the paper.

"You look like a Balthus," William says later. *"Nude with Blue Socks."*

"Really? I must be thirty years too old. Anyway, Balthus. Ugh." She pulls the socks off and throws them on William's nightstand. They're his socks. He must have a dozen pair of navy cashmere socks and he's never asked to have these back. And Charles has never said, Whose are these? They cover Clare almost to the knee, the empty heel swelling gently above her ankle. She wears them all the time.

William lies under the sheets and the comforter, leaving his foot uncovered and resting, like the royal turnip, on a round velvet pillow taken from Isabel's side of the bed.

"Is it better?" Clare asks.

"It is better. I hate for you to have to see it."

Clare shrugs, and William doesn't know if that means that seeing his foot grotesquely swollen and purple cannot diminish her ardor or that her ardor, such as it is, could hardly be diminished.

"I don't mind," she says. She doesn't mind. She didn't mind when her kids were little and projectile vomiting followed weeping chicken pox, which followed thrush and diarrhea; she didn't mind the sharp, dark, powdery smell of her mother's dying or the endless rounds of bedpan and sponge bath. She would have been a great nurse, Clare thought, if the patients never spoke.

"You looked very cute in those socks, I have to tell you." William puts a hand on Clare's stomach.

"I don't know," Clare says. "I think . . . maybe we have to stop this. I think . . ."

William laughs before he sees her face. This is exactly what he has hoped not to hear, and he thought that if she was naked beside him, bare even of his socks and her reading glasses, they would get through the night without having this conversation.

Clare turns on her side to look at him. "You don't think I might have a guilty conscience?"

William sits up and puts on his glasses. He doesn't think Clare has a guilty conscience; he doesn't think she has any kind of conscience at all. She loves Charles, she loves her sons, and she's very fond of William. She'd found herself having sex with William when they were bombing Afghanistan and it seemed the world would end and now they are bombing Iraq and the evening news is horrifying, rather than completely terrifying, and whatever was between them is old hat; it's an anthrax scare, it's Homeland Security; it's something that mattered a great deal for a little while and then not much.

"You might have a guilty conscience. Sometimes people confuse that with a fear of getting caught."

Clare does not say that she would cut William's throat and toss his body in the dump before she would let Charles find them and that there is clearly something wrong with William that he would even mention it.

"I don't want to get a guilty conscience. Let's just say that."

William pushes the socks off the nightstand. There is nothing to be gained by arguing. What they have is nothing to their marriages. Clare to Isabel, he to Charles: two cups of water to the ocean. There's no reason to say: Remember the time you wore my shirt around the motel room like a trench coat and belted it with my tie to go get ice? How about when you sat on top of me in East

Rock Park and you pulled off your T-shirt and the summer light fell through the leaves onto your white shoulders and you bent down close to me, your hair brushing my face, and said, "Those Sherpas ain't got nothin' on me, boy." I have never known another woman who can bear, let alone sing, all of *The Pirates of Penzance,* and who else will ever love me in this deep, narrow, greedy way?

"We'll do whatever you want," he says.

Now Clare laughs. "I don't think so. I think what I want, in this regard, is not possible."

"Probably not."

Oh, put up a fuss, Clare thinks. Throw something. Rise up. Tell me that whatever this costs, however pointless this is, the pleasure of it is so great, your need for me is so tremendous that however this will end—and we are too old not to know that it'll end either this way, with common sense and muted loss and a sad cup of coffee or with something worse in a parking lot somewhere a few months from now, and it's not likely to cover either one of us with glory—it is somehow worth it.

William closes his eyes. I would like it if seeing you would always make me happy, Clare thinks. I would like to have lost nothing along the way.

"What do you think?" she says.

William doesn't open his eyes and Clare thinks, Now I have lost him, as if she has not been trying to lose him without hurting him, for the last hour. She crosses her arms on her chest, in the classic position of going to bed angry (which William may not even recognize—for all Clare knows, he and Isabel talk it out every time, no matter how late), and she thinks, Maybe I just want to hurt him a little, just to watch him take the hit and move on, because he is the kind of man who does. Except in matters of illness, when he sounds like every Jewish man Clare knows, William's Presbyterian stoicism makes for a beautiful, distinctly masculine suffering that Charles can't be bothered with. She uncrosses her arms and puts a hand on William's wide, smooth chest. He looks at her hand and breathes deeply, careful not to shift the comforter toward his foot.

"I don't know," he says. "Farewell, happy fields?"

"You're not helping."

"I'm not trying to help."

"Oh," Clare says.

"It's late," William says.

"I know." Clare rolls toward him.

"Watch out for the turnip."

"I *am*."

Her head is on his chest, her chin above his heart. His hand is deep in her hair. They sleep like this, a tiny tribe, a sliver of marriage, and in their dreams, Clare is married to Charles and they are at Coney Island before it burned down, riding double on number seven in the steeplechase, and they are winning and they keep riding and the stars are as thick as snow. And in their dreams, William is married to Isabel and she brings their daughter home from the hospital, and when William sets her down in the crib, which is much larger and prettier than the one they really had on Elm Street, he sees their baby has small sky-blue wings and little clawed feet.

William kisses the baby's pearly forehead and says, to his wife in the dream and to Clare beside him, It's not the end of the world, darling.

THE OLD IMPOSSIBLE

Clare can't walk.

She has sprained her ankle so badly, it's no better than broken. Marble step, wet leaf, a moment of distraction, and she was pulled up, several feet above the landing and dropped like a bag of laundry, her fingers sliding down the wet iron banister, her feet bending and flopping like fish. Three of her anterior ligaments snapped off as she landed, two small pieces of bone clinging to their ends, and the white rubbery fibers and the tiny triangles of bone continue to float where they should not be, above her ankle's hinge.

Her husband props the crutches up against the coffee table, tilting the handles in Clare's direction, and after he's laid a pillow under her mottled pink-and-blue ankle and a towel over the pillow and a bag of ice over everything, he brings in tea for Clare and her uncle David. He leaves to run errands. Neither of them asks Charles what kind of errands or when he'll be back; he carried and fetched and did for them all morning, and if he had said that he was going off to bet on greyhounds, or try a little Ecstasy, or worse, Clare and David would understand. Clare and David share a strong dislike of being, and caring for, the disabled. David is in Clare and

Charles's house to recover from triple-bypass surgery and to entertain his niece during her period of limited mobility. Mostly, they read together in the living room.

"He *is* sweet," Clare says aloud. It's not what she usually says about her husband. She thinks good things; she thinks interesting, she thinks handsome (the first thousand times he stepped out of the shower, water still flowing down the runnel of his spine, she thought, Jesus, Mary, and Joseph, how can anyone be so beautiful), she thinks he is much nicer than William ever was. William would have shaken his head over her ugly ankle, made his own coffee, and waddled upstairs, leaving her lying on the couch like in *What Ever Happened to Baby Jane?* Clare doesn't think about William every day anymore; she thinks about him mostly when she is falling asleep or when she's about to see him, which will be in the next few minutes. William and Isabel are pulling up to Clare and Charles's front door right now. William struggles with his cane and himself and a bag of nectarines. Isabel gathers up the groceries and a canvas tote of mysteries. She looks away as William rocks himself up and out of the passenger seat.

Uncle David reaches for his tea, which will not be the way he likes it, but he has made up his mind not to complain. The man went to the trouble of making tea. David didn't quite catch what Clare said about Charley. He hopes she isn't complaining. She's no day at the beach, his niece; the sprained ankle has not made her a happier, nicer person. If he were Charley, he would make up pressing business in Baltimore, never mind a few errands downtown.

"This is okay," Uncle David says. "This is fine. He makes a better cup of tea than you do."

"Well, good. Half English. The Magna Carta. Men's shoes. Tea."

"And roast beef," David says, and he is about to add "and sodomy" just to keep the conversational ball rolling, when Isabel he can't remember her last name walks into the room, with bags of things. No one bothered to tell him she was coming. He would have put on a fresh shirt. He might have shaved. She's a good-looking woman, and well read for a real estate agent, and she has that quality, that way of making it clear that she wants him to get what he wants, that makes even plain women—and Isabel is not plain—very attractive. Clare is the more interesting person; as a human being, he'd pick Clare over Isabel, but he can't see how you'd be married to Isabel and chase Clare. It would make no sense, except David does remember chasing, and catching, a big, bushy-haired girl with thighs like Smithfield hams, and after her, chasing an Egyptian ballerina whose kohl ran onto his linen sports coat, so he had to just leave it, streaked and stuffed into a wastebasket, in Grand Central Terminal—all while married to the most beautiful woman in the world, a woman who turned heads until the day she died. He can see his wife and those girls, and a few other women, all rotating delicately in the same shadowy, treacherous light.

"We brought nice things," Isabel says, and kisses them both.

"You smell good," Clare says. Clare doesn't smell good. She smells like rancid butter and wet wool. She smells just like a yak, and her one skimpy shower didn't change that or keep her hair from hanging in limp coils, so that she now has yak ears as well. Uncle David, for whom the word *natty* was invented, who loved to tell people that his late wife always got ready for bed behind a closed door and that as far as he knew, she woke up every morning with brushed hair and a hint of lipstick, should not have to see his niece like this. She's not fit for company, even if it is only Isabel and William, and it never is only Isabel and William. What comes through the door is William as only Clare knows him, naked on a motel bed, sweating like a man with a fever, or cupping her chin in a restaurant and leaning forward with great, premeditated grace to kiss her. And right behind those stolen pictures come Clare's old friends Isabel and William, the four of them playing Monopoly at Cape Cod, and right behind them, her husband, Charles, slicing limes, and behind Charles, their sons, not as they are now, but pink and adorable in their footy pajamas, Danny holding his father's hand, Adam carrying his briefcase. Some of you will simply have to go, Clare wants to say. She smoothes out her ice pack, watches her uncle leer at Isabel, and longs for the thick, amiable hours of Percocet.

William comes in, leaning heavily on a cane, and Clare can't even say hello; the sight of the cane just snaps her mouth shut.

David stands up to shake William's hand and tries to take the bag of nectarines from him. He stands to demonstrate to Isabel—and it's all right for William and Clare to see this, too; he has no objection to either of them noticing—that David and Isabel are the only two people in the room able to get up and down from the furniture whenever they please. William hugs the nectarines.

"What happened to you?" David says.

William is sorry to see David, as he always is. David is the living embodiment of William's bad conscience about sleeping with Clare, and he is not a rueful, forgiving conscience. He is Conscience as a caustic, sensual, dyspeptic old man.

"Nothing much," William says. "How's the heart?"

Isabel says, "Where's Charles?"

"He's running errands," Clare says, and Isabel picks up the tea tray. Privately, Charles and Clare call Isabel The Governess. Isabel purses her lips just a tiny bit as she gathers the cups, and Clare can see her thinking that Charles is out gallivanting—and that would be Isabel's word for it, *gallivanting*—when he should be home supervising Clare, who might try to get herself a glass of water, or worse. It's very pleasant, it is just very warming, to have poor, good Charles on the receiving end of Isabel's disapproval for a change, and Clare throws her shoulders back and down to lengthen her neck and smiles up at William, who smiles back with relief, thinking, She's all right, she's just sick of being Charles's little cripple, as who wouldn't be.

William stands in front of Clare.

"Sit," Clare says, and he sits in the armchair across from David, miles away from Clare, close enough to David to pat him on the knee or, alternatively, smash him in the throat and kill him.

"Sitting," William says. "Shall I roll over, too?"

"What's with the cane?"

"It helps me walk more comfortably." The thought of discussing his rheumatoid arthritis with Clare is disheartening. It is unbearable.

"Oh," Clare says. She looks down at the bag of books Isabel has brought and pulls one out. "God bless Isabel. I like this series."

William smiles politely.

"I never read them," he says. "You know, Isabel goes through hundreds."

"Are you in pain?" Clare says accusingly.

"Yes," he says, and Clare thinks, Oh, God, he's dying.

"I'm just in pain," he says. "I'm not dying."

He shouldn't have come. He should have let Isabel come down by herself, and the women could have had some girl talk and clucked their tongues over the stupidity or cupidity of men, about which he would never argue, and have a few measured glasses of white wine (which is completely untrue to his memory of Clare, who pulled a bottle of Balvenie out of her suitcase when they were still twenty miles from their motel). He's not going to tell Clare, least of all when she's lying there like the little match girl, and certainly least of all while her uncle David sits before them like a cross between Cerberus and Mel Brooks, that he feels like he's been dying for some time. He has not been happy to see daylight any morning that he can remember, and he falls into sleep as if he's been wrapped in chains and tossed overboard.

"I'm not dying," he says again.

"I hope not," Clare says, and shifts her weight to look at him more closely.

"For the love of Jesus," David says. "He's limping, he's not dying. Who are you, Dr. Kevorkian?"

Clare looks at William and smiles. David sees. He could sit here all night, is how David feels, keeping an eye on this big fat smoothie who's just as crazy about Clare as he ever was. Clare's feelings he can't read. She looks old and tired, and in David's experience old and tired is not a breeding ground for illicit love. Not in women. In men, sometimes it makes them try a little harder, to get the woman to chase the old and tired away.

"So, what a pair," David says. "Pair of lame ducks." They shrug, like a pair.

"Since my ankle," Clare says, "I'm only reading about the ambulatory. Cowgirls, lady mountain climbers. Strong-minded women paddling down the Amazon, with their bare hands. Shrunken heads in their lace reticules. Banana leaves on their feet."

"Really," William says.

"Your mother was a great walker," David says. Evoking Clare's mother seems like a good idea. His sister was hell on hanky-panky, and everybody knew it. She threw David out of her house on four different occasions because of hanky-panky. He was sitting on the curb after one Thanksgiving, up to his ass in dead leaves, in front of that house they had in, where, Lake Success, and it was little Clare who came out with his coat, his hat on her head, carrying a beer and a handful of pigs-in-blankets. Life is short, David thinks, and walks out.

"Why don't you just sit by me?" Clare says. "You can provide the elevation." She would ask for more ice, she could actually use some more ice, but if William goes to get it, Isabel will intercept him and want it done properly and bring it herself, knowing that William will bring back three ice cubes in a dripping dish towel. If ice were what Clare wanted most, she would ask Isabel.

William hoists himself up, which he would rather Clare didn't see, and limps over to the couch. She's already seen him limping so there's no help for that, and he holds her feet up and puts himself under them and sinks back onto the sofa, pain gnawing at his hip.

"A lot of activity here," Clare says.

"Oh, yes, quite a ruckus," William says. "I am not going back to that chair anytime soon. David can come back in with Hera and her peacocks, I'm staying on this couch, under these bumpy black-and-blue little feet."

"And the peacocks are for?"

"Peacocks pulled her royal wagon. I have no idea why. She drove everybody crazy. A vigilante about adultery. Most of the myths are about her driving someone insane with her suspicions."

"Gosh, I wonder who wrote those stories. She wasn't wrong, right? Zeus fucked everything. Ship to shore. Ox to goose. Whatever."

"Oh, yes."

Isabel comes into the room and looks at them. There are things she could say, there are plenty of things she could say about her husband, who doesn't like her coat to brush against him when he's driving, who so prefers some space between him and everyone else that he makes reservations for four even when it's the two of them, and who is now making himself into a footrest for their friend Clare. But Clare looks terrible, crumpled and waxy, and her hair, and the two of them are not likely to run off for some brisk lovemaking—how could they and what has it ever been between them but the rubbing up of two broken wings? And Isabel believes that life is what you make it. She adjusts Clare's pillow.

"Do you need anything? David wants to take a little walk, and it's just so gorgeous today—"

Clare and William look out the living room's bay window at the beautiful autumn day, and sigh, as if they have given up all hope of ever walking unaided on beautiful days.

"It's really beautiful," Clare says. I am the worst person in the world, she thinks.

"It is," William says. Go, in Christ's name, he thinks, and take that awful little man with you.

* * *

"We've got an hour to ourselves," William says. "Where should we start?"

"How's Emily?"

"Oh. Fine. She's liking law school—what can I say? You want to talk about our kids?"

"No. What's the matter with your leg?"

"Oh, for fuck's sake. I'd rather talk about the kids. I have bad arthritis, that's all. It acts up. I'm doing what I'm supposed to. Glucosamine chondroitin. Physical therapy. Whole grains. What do you want from me?"

"That's good," Clare says. "I'm glad." She doesn't look glad. She looks chastened and sulky, and she pulls at the corner of her quilt until a wisp of cotton batting appears.

"What's wrong? Comparing yourself to Isabel? Thinking how I'd be curled into a fetal position by now if I were in your hands?"

It is a terrible thing to think and a terrible thing to be seen thinking—Isabel is a better wife than I am—and still Clare's glad that William knows her.

"Jesus, be nice. Nicer."

"I don't have to be nice. Leave the quilt alone. I miss you every day, and we're not even friends anymore."

"We are."

"We are not, and do not dishonor the memory of that beautiful thing by saying otherwise. You know we're not."

Clare wipes her eyes with a corner of the quilt. "Fine. Jesus."

"Less than an hour. If your uncle doesn't come scuttling back to check on us." William picks up Clare's hand and kisses it. He takes a nectarine out of the bag and wraps her hands around it.

"Look at the size of this," Clare says.

Clare twists the nectarine sharply, and it falls into halves, each one a brilliant, glazed yellow with a prickled hot-pink center. The pit falls onto her lap. They eat their halves and watch each other eat, and they drip, just a little, on the quilt. Clare wipes her chin with her wet hands, and then she wipes her face again, on the quilt.

"Napkins would have been good," Clare says.

William shrugs. "I like this," he says. He lifts up the quilt and wipes his hands on Clare's jeans.

"Oh, what is *this,*" she says. If they're going to start acting like the senior-citizen version of *Tom Jones,* smearing their faces with nectarine juice and carrying on, the next thing you know, they'll be hobbling off to motels and looking up positions for the disabled in the sex books. William does not look at all embarrassed; he looks as he always looks: imperturbable, and mildly intrigued, inclined to be benevolent, if no discomfort is involved. Privately, Isabel and Clare call William The Last Emperor and there have been times when Isabel has called Clare to say, "L.E. is driving me mad. Why don't you and Charles come up before I put glass in his cereal?"

"I love a nice nectarine," William says. "My mother made a nectarine tart, I remember. Sliced nectarines and a little brown sugar on top of a brick, just a giant slab of really good pie crust."

William kisses Clare's right hand, then her left, lightly, absent-mindedly, as if in passing.

"What's this?"

"Nothing," William says. "Tell me something else. Tell me a secret."

"Oh, a secret. What a baby. You mean something Charles doesn't know?"

William bites his tongue. He doesn't think Charles knows much, but he could be wrong. He thinks that Charles has been so lucky and so handsome for so long that he's come to think that the world is actually filled with honest men making fair deals and bad people being thwarted by good ones. This is what William prefers to think. Before he slept with her, William thought that Clare had gotten the better half of the bargain. He even said so to Isabel, a few times. Clare is good, spiky company, and she is the very best companion to have in a bad situation. Trouble brings out the cheer beneath her darkness, unlike everyday life, which tends to have the opposite effect, and she holds her liquor like an old Swede, but Charles has to put up with that squinty, unyielding nature, and he does it with real grace, William thinks. In private conversation, the men call Clare The Cactus.

A small boy sticks his head around the doorway and stares at William, rather coolly, from under his long lashes. It is the same look David gives him, now pasted onto a round brown face. William knows he knows the boy, who he is and his place in the world (third grade, grandson of the cleaning lady; Clare likes him; Charles wouldn't know him if he fell over him), but nothing else, like his name or why he is wandering around Clare's house, comes to mind.

"You have company," he says. Small boys are not his department. Small girls are delightful; he would entertain a roomful of little girls, if it were necessary.

"Hey, Nelson." Clare waves to the boy. The boy doesn't say anything.

"Nelson Slater, come on. You've met Mr. Langford before. Last summer."

Nelson nods. Clare sighs. It's not the short, vicious hiss that signals her annoyance. It's not the mild, watery sound she makes when her children call while she's working. It's the sigh of someone settling in for a short, satisfying tussle. If she were upright, Clare would roll up her sleeves.

The boy sits down across from them on the floor. Clare and William smile helplessly. He slides to the floor so easily, he glides right down, and later, he will spring right up. It is a lovely thing to watch, the way gravity barely holds him.

Nelson has come to play checkers. Clare taught him when he was a little kid, and since the accident, Nelson makes a point of coming by every few days, eating the cookies that are always on the coffee table, and fitting in a quick game. His grandmother is collecting old clothes for church, from the garage, and he has fifteen minutes, she says. He might be able to beat Clare in fifteen minutes. It would be better if the fat man went outside, but it's okay—Nelson can just keep his eyes on the board and on Clare's skinny hands, looking closely at the tree of veins on the back of each one, blue branches pointing toward the fingers.

"All right," Clare says, like she's giving in, like she isn't completely ready to kick his ass. "Set it up."

Nelson plays as he always does, death in a bow tie, moving his front line cautiously but already dreaming of the queens slaughtered in their castles, gazing down at his men in terror and admiration, flames leaping orange and blue across their wooden walls.

"Game of Pharaohs," William says. The kid must study Egypt. Mummies and Cleopatra's negritude and the pyramids are what pass for history now. Half an hour left, and they're going to spend it with Clare's little friend.

Nelson pauses in front of one of Clare's pieces. It's not an advantageous jump.

"If you can jump, you must," William says.

"Shut up. He knows."

Clare rolls her eyes so Nelson can see: Ignore him. Nelson nods. He has met some very nice white people, but none of them have been men. He jumps Clare's piece, and she jumps his.

"Watch yourself, young man," Clare says.

"You watch yourself," Nelson says, and laughs.

"Tough guy," William says, and Nelson smiles tightly and looks away.

William sees Nelson's opportunity, an unguarded square that will open up the board for him. You have it, William thinks, you may as well take it. He looks closely at Nelson, as he used to look at his daughter when they played Scrabble. See it, he thinks, see it. Do it. Nelson looks at William as if he's spoken and scans the board. Nelson thinks hard. The man's face is all lit up with wanting Nelson to win. Nelson and the fat man are going to beat Clare, is what Nelson sees. Nelson jumps like crazy, bouncing his man two, then three times and pounding his fists on the floor.

Clare claps.

"Good God. Well. Let's see what I can do with this . . . ruination." It is short work after that. Nelson's men saunter around the board picking off Clare's pieces and when she has trouble reaching to discard them, he scoops them up for her, tossing them in his palm once or twice and laying them on the side of the board in a neat line. They look good, one big red dot after another.

Mrs. Slater honks the horn, which is not what she usually does, but she still has to set up the Jumble Sale and the Baked Goods Table today, and this stop for winter clothes is out of her way. There's no help for it, poor Clare, and it's worth it for the six coats and the many pairs of shoes and the men's suits that will go fast, but this is not something she has time for today.

Sorry to leave the scene of his triumph, Nelson leaps up, to show off for them one more time, graceful and determined as a knight on horseback, and he trips over his untied laces. He puts his hands out toward the floor, but the edge of the coffee table, a sheet of granite, catches him fiercely on the face, and he is down on the rug, screaming in pain and fear and because blood is flowing right into his eye. William very gently puts Clare's feet aside, picks up the boy, and carries him into the kitchen.

"It's okay," he says. "It's okay. It's just blood, it's okay." It may not be okay, but William can see both eyes whole and no bone showing, and if the boy's not blind or crippled, it should be more or less okay.

Clare comes in on her crutches, white around the mouth. She runs cold water and hands an icy dish towel to William, who lays it on the small curvy wound, a little red mouth exhaling blood. Nelson stops screaming. Blood soaks the dish towel.

William says, "A couple of Band-Aids, Clare?" and he pulls the edges of the gash together tightly, so tightly Nelson squirms under him, but William pins him gently and puts the bandages on, butterfly-style.

"Clare, you want to tell his mother, his grandmother, so the poor woman doesn't have a stroke when she sees him?"

Clare wants to stay, but Nelson is nestled on the kitchen counter, resting so comfortably against William, she has to go tell his grandmother the bad news and let William be the hero. (Isabel told her that when baby Emily cried in her crib, Isabel and William would stand, locked hip to hip, in the doorway, each trying to get to her first, each trying to persuade the other that it didn't *matter,* that they just didn't want to *trouble* the other. Clare could not imagine Charles fighting her for the privilege of changing Danny's diaper.) She turns around for a last look, and Nelson is laughing into William's chest; Zeus holding Ganymede beneath his dark wing.

Nelson's grandmother raised three boys and one girl, and an accident that does not involve a broken limb or serious impairment is, as far as she's concerned, the best one can hope for in this treacherous world.

"He's fine," Clare says. "He cut his forehead on that granite coffee table. You know." They have both banged their knees, badly, on that coffee table, and they both watch Nelson walk out the door, followed by William, and they both think that if Clare and Nelson had not been playing checkers, if Nelson had been helping his grandmother in the garage, like the good boy he is, he would not be marching toward them, a wounded boy soldier, with two pale-pink Band-Aids, already darkly bloodstained in their centers, laid above his beautiful eyes. His shirt is ruined.

"I have some plain white T-shirts," Clare says. "I know you're pressed for time." She holds the door for Nelson, and he slides into the backseat to stretch out. His head hurts and there were no cookies and it seems like years ago that he was jumping Clare's pieces and killing her queens where they stood. He puts his head on the pile of coats.

"Don't bleed on those coats, little man. Are you okay? Do you want me to drop you at Auntie's?"

"No." His friends will be at the church. It will look like he has been in a big fight, which he sort of has, and that will be pretty cool. Clare turns the topcoat inside out so the silky lining is against his cheek. No one but Clare would do that for him. "I'm okay. We can go."

"I'll go back and get a T-shirt," Clare says.

Nelson looks at his grandmother in the rearview mirror. He is not going to, and he doesn't think his grandmother will expect him to, or let him, wear one of Clare's own white T-shirts to the church Fall Festival, and a T-shirt that belonged to her husband would fit him like a dress. His grandmother smiles at him in the mirror and shakes her head at Clare.

"Don't you worry—probably some fine shirts in the backseat. Nelson can have his pick. Bye, now." She steps on the gas, like that, and they are off, down the driveway.

Nelson sits up to see Clare waving to him and the fat man giving him a salute. He lies back down on the black silk and replays the last few minutes of the game until they get to church.

"My ankle is killing me," Clare says. "How's your hip?"

"He's a big boy."

"Yes, he is."

"He'll play basketball, I guess."

"Oh, for Christ's sake. Is that what you'd have said about Adam?"

Her son Adam is six-three, and although William is fond of him, the kid is such a sport of nature, he always hoped his Emily, tall and broad-shouldered, would never take a shine to him because their children would have been freaks, some kind of advanced-race humans, who would have lost all control of their huge, flailing limbs.

"Adam? That boy could beat Adam at one-on-one now. I love you."

So it is not a discussion of the limited options for nonwhite children, and it is not a discussion of the hideous fate of young black men, and there's no reason to talk about Adam right now. Clare cannot stop staring at her watch. The second hand is hammering around the dial.

"Oh, I know," she says. "How about a little Percocet? Just a quarter, take the edge off."

"Is that a good idea?" William says. If she had offered him a bottle of almost anything, William would have taken it, but prescription drugs that make you feel better scare the shit out of him.

Clare takes a white pill out of her pocket and bites it in half. She spits half of it back into her hand and swallows.

"Here. Half. You don't have to take it."

William takes it. It seems like an extremely reckless and adolescent thing to do, but he isn't operating any heavy machinery, he isn't driving or running for office, he is just sitting on the couch with his old friend, waiting for his wife to come back.

It dissolves in Clare's throat, leaving a sandy, salty trail. She pulls herself up to William and hugs him.

"You were very good with Nelson. After a while."

"He's a good kid. He was lucky."

"You can't beat lucky," she says.

"We've been lucky. So far," William says.

"We really have." Clare lies down again, her head in William's lap, her feet up on the sofa's arm. William looks down into her eyes, unsmiling, and she looks away.

Maybe, Clare thinks, when Isabel and David return, William will have migrated back to the armchair, reading something high-toned, and I will be resting, attractively, or reading, attractively. And when Charles comes back, he'll find the four of us talking over drinks and eating the goat cheese and crackers that Isabel brought. He'll join us. He'll put his hand on my horrible hair, as if it is nice hair, and he'll sit where William is sitting now.

It is such a golden picture, the five of them. The six of them—

Clare pictures Nelson, too, sitting on the other side of her, in a clean shirt, holding a couple of the cookies she'd forgotten to put out for him before. The light shines on Charles's lovely Nordic hair, a mix of blond and gray, as if the boy and the man will coexist forever, and Isabel is bringing out the best in everyone in her kindest, most encouraging way, as if all she has ever wanted is to help Clare make a nice party, and David tells his stories of Second Avenue, and there is nothing in them, not Great-Aunt Frieda, not the death of little cousin Renee, to make Clare cry, and William tells her that he will love her forever, that nothing has been lost, after all, and he mouths the words so that no one can hear him, but her, of course, and it is so beautiful, so drenched in the lush, streaming light of what is not, she closes her eyes to see it better and falls asleep.

William relaxes. There really is nothing more to do. He can just close his eyes, too. Clare's hair fans out across his lap. Her hands press his to her chest. The objects in the room darken, until it is a black reef from couch to table to chair, and no one turns on the light. William and Clare sleep, as if it is a quiet night in their own home, as if they are lying naked and familiar in their own bed.

COMPASSION AND MERCY

For JOB

No power.

The roads were thick with pine branches and whole birch trees, the heavy boughs breaking off and landing on top of houses and cars and in front of driveways. The low, looping power lines coiled onto the road, and even from their bedroom window, Clare could see silver branches dangling in the icy wires. Highways were closed. Classes were canceled. The phone didn't work. The front steps were slippery as hell.

William kept a fire going in the living room and Clare toasted rye bread on the end of fondue forks for breakfast, and in the early afternoon, they wrapped cheese sandwiches in tin foil and threw them into the embers for fifteen minutes. William was in charge of dinner and making hot water for Thai ginger soup-in-a-bowl. They used the snow bank at the kitchen door to chill the Chardonnay.

They read and played Scrabble and at four o'clock, when daylight dropped to a deep indigo, Clare lit two dozen candles and they got into their pile of quilts and pillows.

"All right," William said. "Let's have it. You're shipwrecked on a desert island. Who do you want to be with—me or Nelson Slater?"

"Oh my God," Clare says. "Nelson. Of course."

"Good choice. He did a great job with the firewood."

William kept the fire going all night. Every hour, he had to roll sideways and crouch and then steady himself and then pull himself up with his cane and then balance himself, and because Clare was watching and worried, he had to do it all with the appearance of ease. Clare lay in the dark and tried to move the blankets far to one side so they wouldn't tangle William's feet.

"You're not actually helping," he said. "I know where the blankets are, so I can easily step over them. And then, of course, you move them."

"I feel bad," Clare said.

"I'm going to break something if you keep this up."

"Let me help," Clare said.

When the cold woke them, Clare handed William the logs. They talked about whether or not it was worth it to use the turkey carcass for soup and if they could really make a decent soup in the fireplace. William said that people had cooked primarily in hearths until the late eighteenth century. William told Clare about his visit to his cardiologist and the possible levels of fitness William could achieve. ("A lot of men your age walk five miles a day," the doctor said. "My father-in-law got himself a personal trainer, and he's eighty.") Clare said maybe they could walk to the diner on weekends. They talked about Clare's sons, Adam and Danny, and their wives and the two grandchildren and they talked about William's daughter, Emily, and her pregnancy and the awful man she'd married ("I'd rather she'd taken the veil," William said. "Little Sisters of Gehenna"). When the subject came up, William and Clare said nice things about the people they used to be married to.

* * *

It had taken William and Clare five years to end their marriages. William's divorce lawyer was the sister of one of William's old friends. She was William's age, in a sharp black suit and improbably black hair and bloodred nails. Her only concession to age was black patent flats, and William was sure that most of her life, this woman had been stalking and killing wild game in stiletto heels.

"So," she said. "You've been married thirty-five years. Well, look, Dr. Langford—"

" 'Mister' is fine," William said. " 'William' is fine."

" 'Bill'?" the woman said and William shook his head no and she smiled and made a note.

"Just kidding. It's like this. Unless your wife is doing crack cocaine or having sex with young girls and barnyard animals, what little you have will be split fifty-fifty."

"That's fine, Mrs. Merrill," William said.

"Not really," the woman said. "Call me Louise. Your wife obviously got a lawyer long before you did. I got a fax today, a list of personal property your wife believes she's entitled to. Oil paintings, a little jewelry, silverware."

"That's fine. Whatever it is."

"It's not fine. But let's say you have no personal attachment to any of these items. And let's say it's all worth about twenty thousand dollars. Let's have her give you twenty thousand dollars, and you give her the stuff. There's no reason for us to just roll over and put our paws up in the air."

"Whatever she wants," William said. "You should know, I'm not having sex with a graduate student. Or with porn stars."

"I believe you," Mrs. Merrill said. "You may as well tell me—it'll all come out in the wash. Who are you having sex with?"

"Her name is Clare Wexler. She teaches. She's a very fine teacher. She makes me laugh. She can be a difficult person," he said, beaming, as if he were detailing her beauty. "You'd like her." William wiped his eyes.

"All right," said Louise Merrill. "Let's get you hitched before we're all too old to enjoy it."

When they could finally marry, Clare called her sons.

Danny said, "You might want a prenup. I'm just saying."

Adam said, "Jeez, I thought Isabel was your friend."

William called Emily and she said, "How can you do this to me? I'm trying to get pregnant," and her husband, Kurt, had to take the phone because she was crying so hard. He said, "We're trying not to take sides, you know."

Three days after the storm had passed, classes resumed, grimy cars filled slushy roads, and Clare called both of her sons to say they were essentially unharmed.

"What do you mean, 'essentially'?" Danny said, and Clare said, "I mean my hair's a mess and I lost at Scrabble seventeen times and William's back hurts from sleeping near the fireplace. I mean, I'm absolutely and completely fine. I shouldn't have said 'essentially.' "

William laughed and shook his head when she hung up.

"They must know me by now," Clare said.

"I'm sure they do," William said, "but knowing and understanding are two different things. *Verstehen und erklären.*"

"Fancy talk," Clare said, and she kissed his neck and the bald top of his head and the little red dents behind his ears, which came from sixty-five years of wearing glasses. "I have to go to Baltimore tomorrow. Remember?"

"Of course," William said.

Clare knew he'd call her the next day to ask about dinner, about Thai food or Cuban or would she prefer scrambled eggs and salami and then when she said she was on her way to Baltimore, William would be, for just a quick minute, crushed and then crisp and English.

They spoke while Clare was on the train. William had unpacked his low-salt, low-fat lunch. ("Disgusting," he'd said. "Punitive.") Clare had gone over her notes for her talk on *Jane Eyre* ("In which I will reveal my awful, retrograde underpinnings") and they made their nighttime phone date for ten P.M., when William would be still at his desk at home and Clare would be in her bed at the University Club.

Clare called William every half hour from ten until midnight and then she told herself that he must have fallen asleep early. She called him at his university office, on his cell phone, and at home. She called him every fifteen minutes from seven A.M. until her talk and she began calling him again, at eleven, as soon as her talk was over. She begged off the faculty lunch and said that her husband wasn't well and that she was needed at home; her voice shook and no one doubted her.

On the train, Clare wondered who to call. She couldn't ask Emily, even though she lived six blocks away; she couldn't ask a pregnant woman to go see if her father was all right. By the time she'd gotten Emily to understand what was required, and where the house key was hidden, and that there was no real cause for alarm, Emily would be sobbing and Clare would be trying not to scream at Emily to calm the fuck down. Isabel was the person to call, and Clare couldn't call her. She could imagine Isabel saying, "Of course, Clare, leave it to me," and driving down from Boston to sort things out; she'd make the beds, she'd straighten the pictures, she'd gather all the overdue library books into a pile and stack them near the front door. She'd scold William for making them all worry and then she would call Clare back, to say that all broken things had been put right.

Clare couldn't picture what might have happened to William. His face floated before her, his large, lovely face, his face when he was reading the paper, his face when he'd said to her, "I *am* sorry," and she'd thought, Oh, Christ, we're breaking up again; I thought we'd go until April at least, and he'd said, "You are everything to me—I'm afraid we have to marry," and they cried so hard, they had to sit down on the bench outside the diner and wipe each other's faces with napkins.

Clare saw that the man in the seat across from her was smiling uncertainly; she'd been saying William's name. Clare walked to the little juncture between cars and called Margaret Slater, her former cleaning lady. There was no answer. Margaret's grandson Nelson didn't get home until three so Margaret might be running errands for another two hours. They pulled into Penn Station. If Margaret had a cell phone, Clare didn't know the number. Clare called every half hour, home and then Margaret's number, leaving messages and timing herself, reading a few pages of the paper between calls. Goddammit, Margaret, she thought. You're retired. Pick up the fucking phone.

Clare pulled into their driveway just as the sun was setting and Margaret pulled in right after her. Water still dripped from the gutters and the corners of the house and it would all freeze again at night.

"Oh, Clare," Margaret said, "I just got your messages. I was out of the house all day. I'm so sorry."

"It's all right," Clare said, and they both looked up at the light in William's window. "He probably unplugged the phone."

"They live to drive us crazy," Margaret said.

Clare scrabbled in the bottom of her bag for the house key, furiously tossing tissues and pens and Chap Sticks and quarters onto the walk, and thinking with every toss, What's your hurry? This is your last moment of not knowing, stupid, slow down. But her hands moved fast, tearing the silk lining of the bag until she saw, out of the corner of her eye, a brass house key sitting in Margaret's flat, lined palm. Clare wanted to sit down on the porch and wait for someone else to come. She opened the door and she wanted to turn around and close it behind her.

They should call his name, she thought. It's what you do when you come into your house and you haven't been able to reach your husband, you go, *William, William, darling, I'm home,* and then he pulls himself out of his green leather desk chair and comes to the top of the stairs, his hair standing straight up and his glasses on the end of his nose. He says, relief and annoyance clearly mixed together, *Oh, darling, you didn't call, I waited for your call.* And then you say, *I* did *call, I called all night, but the phone was off the hook, you had the phone off,* and he says that he certainly did not and Margaret watches, bemused. She disapproved of the divorce (she all but said, I always thought Charles would leave you, not the other way around) but gave herself over on the wedding day, when she brought platters of deviled eggs and put Nelson in a navy-blue suit, and cried, shyly.

"Fulgent," William said after the ceremony, and he said it several times, a little drunk on Champagne. "Absolutely *fulgent.*" It wouldn't have mattered if no one had been there, but everyone except William's sister had been, and they got in one elegant fox-trot before William's ankle acted up. William will call down, "I'm so sorry we inconvenienced you, Mrs. Slater," and Margaret will shake her head fondly and go, and you drop your coat and bag in the hall and he comes down the stairs, slowly, careful with his ankle, and he makes tea to apologize for having scared the shit out of you.

Margaret waited. As much as she wanted to help, it wasn't her house or her husband and Clare had been in charge of their relationship for the last twenty years; this was not the moment to take the lead. Clare walked up the stairs and right into their bedroom, as if William had phoned ahead and told her what to expect. He was lying on the bed, shoes off and fully dressed, his hand on *Jane Eyre,* his eyes closed, and his reading glasses on his chest. (" 'He is not to them what he is to me,' " Jane thought. " 'While I breathe and think I must love him.' ") Clare lay down next to him, murmuring, until Margaret put her hand on Clare's shoulder and asked if she should call the hospital or someone.

"I have no idea," Clare said, lying on the bed beside William, staring at the ceiling. These things get done, Clare thought, whether you know what you're doing or not. The hospital is called, the funeral home is contacted, the body is removed, with some difficulty, because he was a big man and the stairs are old and narrow. Your sons and daughters-in-law call everyone who needs to be called, including the terrible sister in England who sent them a note and a chipped vase, explaining that she could not bring herself to attend a wedding that so clearly should not be taking place.

Margaret comes back the next day and makes up one of the boys' bedrooms for you, just in case, but when your best friend flies in from Cleveland, you are lying in your own room, wrapped in William's bathrobe, and you wear his robe and his undershirt while she sits across from you, her sensible shoes right beside William's wing tips, and she helps you decide chapel or funeral home, lunch or brunch, booze or wine, and who will speak. Your sons and their wives and the babies come and it's no more or less terrible to have them in the house. You move slowly and carefully, swimming through a deep but traversable river of shit. You must not inhale, you must not stop, you must not stop for anything at all. Destroyed, untouchable, you can lie down on the other side when they've all gone home.

Clare was careful during the funeral. She didn't listen to anything that was said. She saw Isabel sitting with Emily and Kurt, a little cluster of Langfords; Isabel wore a gray suit and held Emily's hand and she left as soon as the service ended. At the house, Clare imagined Isabel beside her; she imagined herself encased in Isabel. Even in pajamas, suffering a bad cold, Isabel moved like a woman in beautiful silk. Clare made an effort to move that way. She thanked people in Isabel's pleasant, governessy voice. Clare straightened Danny's tie with Isabel's hand and then wiped chocolate fingerprints off the back of a chair. Clare used Isabel to answer every question and to make plans to get together with people she had no intention of seeing. She hugged Emily the way Isabel would have, with a perfect degree of appreciation for Emily's pregnant and furious state. Clare went upstairs and lay down on the big bed and cried into the big, tailored pillows William used for reading in bed. Clare held his reading glasses like a rosary. Clare walked over to the dresser and took out one of William's big Irish linen handkerchiefs and blotted her face with it. (Clare and Isabel did their dressers the same way, William said: odds and ends in the top drawer, then underwear, then sweaters, then jeans and T-shirts and white socks. Clare put William's almost empty bottle of Tabac in her underwear drawer.) She rearranged their two unlikely stuffed animals.

"Oh, rhino and pecker bird," William had said. That's how he saw them, and two years ago Clare had found herself in front of a fancy toy store in Guilford on a spring afternoon and found herself buying a very expensive plush gray rhino and a velvety little brown-and-white bird and putting the pair on their bed that night.

"You're not so tough," William had said.

"I was," Clare said. "You've ruined me."

Clare wanted to talk with Isabel about Emily; they used to talk about her all the time. Once, after William's second heart attack, when William was still Isabel's husband, Isabel and Clare were playing cards in William's hospital room and Emily and Kurt had just gone off to get sandwiches and Clare had stumbled over something nice to say about Kurt, and Isabel slapped down her cards and said, "Say what you want. He's dumb in that awful preppy way and a Republican and if he says, 'No disrespect intended,' one more time, I'm going to set him on fire." William said, *"De gustibus non est dis-*

putandum," which he said about many things, and Isabel said, "That doesn't help, darling."

Clare looked at William's lapis cuff links and at the watch she'd given him when they were in the third act of their affair. "You can't give me a watch," he'd said. "I already have a perfectly good one." Clare took his watch off his wrist, laid it on the asphalt, and drove over it, twice. "There," she'd said. "Terrible accident, you were so careless. You had to replace it." William took that beautiful watch she'd bought him out of the box and kissed her in the parking lot of a Marriott halfway between his home and hers. He'd worn it every day until last Thursday. Clare walked downstairs holding William's jewelry, and when she passed her sons pouring wine for people, she dropped the watch into Danny's pocket. Adam turned to her and said, "Mom, do you want a few minutes alone?" and Clare realized the time upstairs had done her no good at all. She laid the lapis cuff links in Adam's free hand. "William particularly wanted you to have these," she said, and Adam looked surprised—as well he might, Clare thought.

Clare took the semester off. She spent weeks in the public library, crying and wandering up and down the mystery section, looking for something she hadn't read. A woman she didn't know popped out from behind the stacks and handed her a little ivory pamphlet, the pages held together with a dark-blue silk ribbon. On the front it said, GOD NEVER GIVES US MORE THAN WE CAN BEAR. The woman ran off and Clare caught the eye of the librarian, who mouthed the words "ovarian cancer." Clare carried it with her to the parking lot and looked over her shoulder to make sure the woman was gone and then she tossed it in the trash.

After the library, Clare went to the coffeehouse or to the

Turkish restaurant, where they knew how to treat widows. Every evening at six, men would spill out of the church across the street from the coffeehouse. A few would smoke in the vestibule and a few more would come in and order coffee and a couple of cookies and sit down to play chess. They were not like the chess players Clare had known.

One evening, one of the older men, with a tidy silver crew cut and pants yanked up a little too high, approached Clare. (William had dressed beautifully. Clare and Isabel used to talk about how beautifully he dressed; Clare said he dressed the way the Duke of Windsor would have if he'd been a hundred pounds heavier and not such a weenie and Isabel said, "That's wonderful. May I tell him?")

The man said gently, "Are you waiting for the meeting?"

Clare said, in her Isabel voice, that it was very kind of him to ask, but there was no meeting she was waiting for.

He said, "Well, I see you here a lot. I thought maybe you were trying to decide whether or not to go to the next meeting."

Clare said that she hadn't made up her mind, which could have been true. She could just as soon have gone to an AA meeting as to a No Rest for the Weary meeting or a People Sick of Life meeting. And Clare did know something about drinking, she thought. Sometime after she and William had decided, for the thousandth time, that their affair was a terrible thing, that their love for their spouses was much greater than their love for each other, that William and Isabel were *suited,* just like Charles and Clare were suited, and that the William and Clare thing was nothing more than some odd summer lightning that would pass as soon as the season changed, Clare found herself having three glasses of wine every night. Her goal, every night, was to climb into bed early, exhausted and tipsy, and fall deeply asleep before she could say anything to Charles about William. It was her version of One Day at a Time, and it worked for two years, until she woke up one night, crying and saying William's name into her pillow over and over again. Clare didn't think that that was the kind of reckless behavior that interested the people across the street.

The man put "AA for the Older Alcoholic" in front of Clare and said, "You're not alone."

Clare said, "That is *so* not true."

She kept the orange-and-gray pamphlet on her kitchen table for a few weeks, in case anyone dropped in, because it made her laugh, the whole idea. Her favorite part (she had several, especially the stoic recitation of ruined marriages, dead children, estranged children, alcoholic children, multiple car accidents—pedestrian and vehicular—forced resignations, outright firings, embezzlements, failed suicides, diabetic comas), her absolute favorite in the category of the telling detail, was an old woman carrying a fifth of vodka hidden in a skein of yarn. Clare finally put the pamphlet away so it wouldn't worry Nelson when he came for Friday night dinner. Margaret Slater dropped him off at six and picked him up at eight-thirty, which gave her time for bingo and Nelson and Clare time to eat and play checkers or cribbage or Risk.

Nelson Slater didn't know that William's Sulka pajamas were still under Clare's pillow, that the bedroom still smelled like his cologne (and that Clare had bought two large bottles of it and sprayed the room with it, every Sunday), that his wing tips and his homely black sneakers were in the bottom of the bedroom closet. He knew that William's canes were still in the umbrella stand next to the front door and that the refrigerator was filled with William's favorite foods (chicken-liver pâté, cornichons, pickled beets, orange marmalade, and Zingerman's bacon bread) and there were always two or three large Tupperware containers of William's favorite dinners, which Clare made on Friday, when Nelson came over, and then divided in halves or quarters for the rest of the week. Nelson didn't mind. He had known and loved Clare most of his young life, and he understood old-people craziness. His great-aunt believed that every event in the Bible actually happened and left behind physical evidence you could buy, like the splinter from

Noah's Ark she kept by her bed. His Cousin Chick sat on the back porch, shooting the heads off squirrels and chipmunks and reciting poetry. Nelson had known William Langford since he was five, and Nelson had gotten used to him. Mr. Langford was a big man with a big laugh and a big frown. He gave Nelson credit for who he was and what he did around the house and he paid Nelson, which Clare never remembered to do. (A man has to make a living, Mr. Langford had said one time, and Nelson did like that.) Nelson liked the Friday night dinners, and unless Clare started doing something really weird, like setting three places at the table, he'd keep coming over.

"Roast pork with apples and onions and a red wine sauce. And braised red cabbage. And Austrian apple cake. How's that?"

Nelson shrugged. Clare was always a good cook, but almost no one knew it. When he was six years old and eating gingerbread in the Wexler kitchen one afternoon, Mr. Wexler came home early. He reached for a piece of the warm gingerbread and Nelson told him that Clare had just baked it and Wexler looked at him in surprise. "Mrs. Wexler doesn't really cook," he said, and Nelson had gone on eating and thought, She does for me, Mister.

Clare put the pork and apples on Nelson's plate and poured them both apple cider. When Nelson lifted the fork to his mouth and chewed and then sighed and smiled, happy to be loved and fed, Clare had to leave the kitchen for a minute.

After a year, everything was much the same. Clare fed Nelson on Friday nights, she taught half-time, she wept in the shower, and at the end of every day, she put on one of William's button-down shirts and a pair of his socks and settled down with a big book of William's or an English mystery. When the phone rang, Clare jumped.

"Clare, how are you?"

"Good, Lauren. How are you? How's Adam?"

Her daughter-in-law would not be deflected. She tried to get her husband to call his mother every Sunday night but when he didn't (and Clare could just hear him, her sweet boy, passive as granite: "She's okay, Lauren. What do you want me to do about it?"), Lauren, who was properly brought up, made the call.

"We'd love for you to visit us, Clare."

I bet, Clare thought. "Oh, not until the semester ends, I can't. But you all could come out here. Anytime."

"It really wouldn't be suitable."

Clare said nothing.

"I mean, it just wouldn't," Lauren said, polite and stubborn.

Clare felt sorry for her. Clare wouldn't want herself for a mother-in-law, under the best of circumstances.

"I'd love to have you visit," Clare said. This wasn't exactly true but she would certainly rather have them in her house than be someplace that had no William in it. "The boys' room is all set, with the bunk beds and your room, of course, for you and Adam. There's plenty of room and I hear Cirque du Soleil will be here in a few weeks." Clare and Margaret will take Nelson, before he's too old to be seen in public with two old ladies.

Lauren's voice dropped. Clare knew she was walking from the living room, where she was watching TV and folding laundry, into a part of the house where Adam couldn't hear her.

"It doesn't matter how much room there is. Your house is like a mausoleum. How am I supposed to explain that to the boys, Clare? Am I supposed to say Grandma loved Grandpa William so much she keeps every single thing he ever owned or read or *ate* all around her?"

"I don't mind if that's what you want to tell them."

In fact, I'll tell them myself, Little Miss Let's-Call-a-Spade-a-Gardening-Implement, Clare thought, and she could hear William saying, "Darling, you are as clear and bright as vinegar but not everyone wants their pipes cleaned."

"I don't want to tell them that. I want—really, we all want—for you just to begin to, oh, you know, just to get on with your life a little bit."

Clare said, and she thought she never sounded more like Isabel, master of the even, elegant tone, "I completely understand, Lauren, and it is very good of you to call."

Lauren put the boys on and they said exactly what they should: Hi, Grandma, thanks for the Legos. (Clare put Post-its next to the kitchen calendar, and at the beginning of every month, she sent an educational toy to each grandchild, so no one could accuse her of neglecting them.) Lauren walked back into the living room and forced Adam to take the phone. Clare said to him, before he could speak, "I'm all right, Adam. Not to worry," and he said, "I know, Mom," and Clare asked about his work and Lauren's classes and she asked about Jason's karate and the baby's teeth, and when she could do nothing more, she said, "Oh, I'll let you go now, honey," and she sat on the floor, with the phone still in her hand.

One Sunday, Danny called and said, "Have you heard about Dad?" And Clare's heart clutched, just as people describe, and when she didn't say anything, Danny cleared his throat and said, "I thought you might have heard. Dad's getting married." Clare was so relieved she was practically giddy. "Oh, wonderful," she said. "That nice, tall woman who golfs?" Danny laughed. Almost everything you could say about his future stepmother pointed directly to the ways she was not his mother—particularly nice, tall, and golfs. Clare got off the phone and sent Charles and his bride—she didn't remember her name, so she sent it to Mr. and Mrs. Charles Wexler, which had a nice old-fashioned ring to it—a big pretty Tiffany vase of the kind she'd wanted when she married Charles.

The only calls Clare made were to Isabel. She called in the early evening, before Isabel turned in. (There was nothing she didn't know about Isabel's habits. They'd shared a beach house three summers in a row and she'd slept in their guest room in Boston a dozen times. She knew Isabel's taste in linens, in kitchens, in moisturizer and makeup and movies. There was not a single place on earth that you could put Clare that she couldn't point out to you what would suit Isabel and what would not.) She dialed her number, William's old number, and when Isabel answered, she hung up, of course.

Clare called Isabel about once a week, after watching *Widow's Walk,* the most repulsive and irresistible show she'd ever seen. Three, sometimes four women sat around and said things like, "It's not an ending; it's a beginning." What made it bearable to Clare was that the women were all ardent Catholics and not like her, except the discussion leader, who was so obviously Jewish and from the Bronx that Clare had to Google her and discover that she had a Ph.D. in philosophical something and converted to Catholicism after a personal tragedy. Clare got to hear a woman who sounded a lot like her great-aunt Frieda say, "I pray for all widows, and we must all keep on with our faith and never forget that Jesus meets every need." Clare waited for the punch line, for the woman to yank her cross off her neck and say, "And if you believe that, *bubbeleh,* I've got a bridge I'd like to sell you," but she never did. She did sometimes say, in the testing, poking tone of a good rabbi, "Isn't it interesting that so many women saints came to their sainthood through being widows? They were poor and desperate, alone in the world with no protection, but the sisters took them in and even educated their children. Isn't it *interesting* that widowhood led them to become saints and extraordinary women, to know themselves and Jesus better?" The other widows, the real Catholics, didn't look interested at all. The good-looking one, in a red suit and red high heels, kept reminding everyone that she was very recently widowed (and young, and pretty) and the other two, a garden gnome in baggy pants and black sneakers that didn't touch the floor and a tall woman in a frilly blouse with her glasses taped together at the bridge, talked, in genuinely heartbroken tones, about their lives now that they were alone. They rarely mentioned their husbands, although the gnome did say, more than once, that if she could forgive her late husband, anyone could forgive anyone.

Clare dials, as soon as the organ music dies down, and Isabel picks up after one ring. Clare doesn't speak.

"Clare?"

Clare sighs. Hanging up was bad enough.

"Isabel."

Isabel sighs as well.

"I saw Emily a few weeks ago. I dropped off a birthday present for baby Charlotte. She's beautiful. Emily seems very happy. I mean, not to see me, but in general."

"Yes, she told me."

"I shouldn't have gone."

"Well. If you want to offer a relationship and generous gifts, it's up to Emily. Kurt's mother's dead. I guess it depends on how many grandmothers Emily wants Charlotte to have, regardless of who they are." There was no one like Isabel.

"I guess it does. I mean, I'm not going to presume. I'm not going to drop in all the time with a box of rugelach and a hand-knit sweater."

"I wouldn't think so. Clare—"

"Oh, Isabel, I miss you."

"Good night, Clare."

When Clare gets off the phone, there's a raccoon in her kitchen, on the counter. It, although Clare immediately thinks He, is eating a slice of bacon bread. He's holding it in his small, nimble, and very human black hands. He looks at her over the edge of the bread, like a man peering over his glasses. A fat, bold, imperturbable man with a twinkle in his dark eyes.

Even though she knows better, even though William would

have been very annoyed at her for doing so, Clare says, softly, "William."

The raccoon doesn't answer and Clare smiles. She wouldn't have wanted the raccoon to say, "Clare." Because then she would have had to call her boys and have herself committed, and although this is not the life she hoped to have, it's certainly better than being in a psychiatric hospital. The raccoon has started on his second slice of bacon bread. Clare would like to put out the orange marmalade and a little plate of honey. William never ate peanut butter, but Clare wants to open a jar for the raccoon. She's read that they love peanut butter, and she doesn't want him to leave.

In an ideal world, the raccoon would give Clare advice. He would speak to her like Quan Yin, the Buddhist goddess of compassion and mercy. Or he would speak to her like Saint Paula, the patron saint of widows, about whom Clare has heard so much lately.

Clare says, without moving, "And why is Saint Paula a saint? She dumps her four kids at a convent, after the youngest dies. She runs off to *hajira* with Saint Jerome. How is that a saint? You've got shitty mothers all over America who would love to dump their kids and travel."

The raccoon nibbles at the crust.

"Oh, it's very hard," Clare says, sitting down slowly and not too close. "Oh, I miss him so much. I didn't know. I didn't know that I would be like this, that this is what happens when you love someone like that. I had no idea. No one says, There's no happy ending at all. No one says, If you could look ahead, you might want to stop now. I know, I know, I know I was lucky. I was luckier than anyone to have had what I had. I know now. I do, really."

The raccoon picks up two large crumbs and tosses them into his mouth. He scans the counter and the canisters and looks closely at Clare. He hops down from the counter to the kitchen stool and onto the floor and strolls out the kitchen door.

* * *

Clare told Nelson about the raccoon and they encouraged him with heels of bread and plastic containers of peanut butter leading up the kitchen steps, but he didn't come back. She told Margaret Slater, who said she was lucky not to have gotten rabies, and she told Adam and Danny, who said the same thing. She bought a stuffed-animal raccoon with round black velvet paws much nicer than the actual raccoon's, and she put him on her bed with the rhino and the little bird and William's big pillows. She told little Charlotte raccoon stories when she came to babysit (how could Emily say no to a babysitter six blocks away and free and generous with her time?). She even told Emily, who paused and said, with a little concern, that raccoons could be very dangerous.

"I don't know if you heard," Emily said. "My mother's getting married. A wonderful man."

Clare bounced Charlotte on her knee. "Oh, good. Then everyone is happy."

Opening the Hands Between Here and Here

On the dark road, only the weight of the rope.
Yet the horse is there.

—Jane Hirshfield

BETWEEN HERE AND HERE

For ESBL

I had always planned to kill my father. When I was ten, I drew a picture of a grave with ALVIN LOWALD written on the tombstone, on the wall behind my dresser. From time to time, I would add a spray of weeds or a creeping vine. By the time I was in junior high, there were trees hung with kudzu, cracks in the granite, and a few dark daisies springing up. Once, when my mother wouldn't let me ride my bike into town, I wrote, *Peggy Lowald is a fat stupid cow* behind the dresser but I went back the same day and scribbled over it with black Magic Marker because most of the time I did love my mother and I knew she loved me. The whole family knew that my mother's feelings were Sensitive and Easily Hurt. My father said so, all the time. My father's feelings were also sensitive, but not in a way that I understood the word, at ten; it might be more accurate to say that he was extremely responsive. My brother, Andy, drew cartoon weather maps of my father's feelings: dark clouds of I Hate You, giving way to the sleet of Who Are You, pierced by bolts of Black Rage.

Most of the mothers in our neighborhood were housewives, like my mother. But my mother was really a very good cook and a very accomplished hostess, even if the things she made and the way she entertained is not how I would have done it (red, white, and blue frilled toothpicks in lamb sausage pigs-in-blankets on the Fourth of July, trays of deviled eggs and *oeufs en gelée*—with tiny tulips of chive and egg yolk decorating each *oeuf*—to celebrate spring). My mother worked hard at what she considered her job, with no thanks from us and no pay, aside from the right to stay home.

Five minutes before the start of a cocktail party or bridge night, my father would make himself comfortable on the living room couch, dropping cigar ash on the navy-blue velvet cushions, or he'd stand in the kitchen in his underwear, reading the newspaper while my mother and I put out platters and laid hors d'oeuvres around him. Sometimes, he'd sit down at the kitchen table and open the newspaper wide, lowering it almost to the tabletop, so we'd have to move the serving dishes to the counter. One July Fourth, when I was about twelve and Andy was ten, my father picked up an angel on horseback as my mother was carrying the tray past him. "What is this, shit on a stick," he said, and knocked the whole plate out of her hands, and then there we were, my mother and Andy and me, scrabbling to grab the hot, damp, oily little things from under the sideboard and out of the ficus plants. My father picked up a couple and put them in my mother's apron pocket, saying, "You kids crack me up." He was still chuckling when the doorbell rang and my mother went back into the kitchen and Andy and I went to our rooms, and he was still smiling when he opened the door for Mr. and Mrs. Rachlin, who were always the first.

When I got to college, other people's stories were much worse. A girl down the hall told her parents she was pregnant her senior year of high school and they drove her to a home for unwed mothers on Christmas Eve and moved out of town. A boy I liked had a long, ropy scar on his back from a belt; my roommate had cigarette burns on her instep. Gross cruelty with canapés and bad temper hardly seemed worth mentioning. (Amazingly, my brother chose to come out to both my parents his sophomore year. He said my mother wiped away a quick tear and hugged him and thanked him for telling her, and just as I was about to say, Good for Mom, Andy told me that Dad had lowered his newspaper, poked him in the stomach, and said, "A fat fag? Not much fun in that," and gone back to his paper.) In law school, at night, over drinks, everyone told funnier family stories and no one pulled up their shirt or rolled down their socks to show their scars. When it got really late, a few guys told my kind of stories and then they would say, frankly or sadly or fondly, that these things happened only when the old man had been drinking.

My father didn't drink. He had a glass of white wine at the cocktail parties, and in the summertime, when he was grilling hamburgers, he'd have a beer. One glass of wine. One beer. I didn't have to watch to see if this was the drink that turned Good Daddy into Bad Daddy; there was no slow, nightly disintegration of the self. I never had to tiptoe around Daddy Sleeping It Off, because my father took a four-mile walk every day, and if it rained, he spent an hour on the rowing machine in the basement. Andy and I always caught the late bus home, and after dinner we did our homework in our rooms, and when I got a stereo for my fifteenth birthday, Andy and I would lie on my floor and listen to loud rock and roll, very, very quietly.

"Am I talking to myself, goddammit?" my father said one night at dinner, and in the silence Andy said, "I guess so, Dad," and I laughed, which I knew was a mistake even as my lips parted, and my father stood up, hands wandering from head to head, unable to choose which one of us to kill first. I pushed Andy under the table and pulled him down the hall to my bedroom and pressed the lousy little push-button lock on the door. My father threw our dinners on the floor. My mother was still sitting at the table, trying to be calm, which did sometimes work, and sometimes not, as when he took her two favorite silk scarves and used them to stake his tomato plants, or another time, famous in our family, when he drove her car to a used-car lot, sold it, and took a cab home with a bag of cash in one hand and a box of pizza in the other.

"You could kill yourself on these creamed onions," he said, stepping over them, and I could hear my mother murmuring agreement and I heard him say, pleasantly, that sometimes the kids were too smart for their own damned good. I heard my mother agree with that, too, and my father said he would catch the tail end of the news. About an hour later, my mother knocked on my door and handed us two plates of plastic-wrapped dinner, the meat-loaf slices reconstructed and carrot-raisin salad instead of the creamed onions.

I dated a few boys of the kind you'd expect from a girl like me with a father like that, with no real harm done, and in the middle of law school, I met Jay Johnson. I won him the way poor people occasionally win the lottery: Shameless perseverance and embarrassingly dumb luck, and every time I see one of those sly, toothless, beaten-down souls on TV holding a winning ticket, I think, Go, team. When we went to his family in Wisconsin to announce our engagement (on our side, my mother took us both to lunch at her favorite restaurant on Northern Boulevard and my father met Jay the night before the wedding), I found a second family; the Johnson women were good, tireless cooks and all the men, including mine, could build you a willow rocking chair or a pair of handsome nightstands in just a few afternoons. And, as it happened, almost all of them were recovering alcoholics. I fell in love with them all. The Johnsons drank coffee and Diet Coke all day (even the toddlers had highballs of fresh milk with a splash of black coffee at breakfast) and at cocktail hour my mother-in-law served Ritz crackers with cheddar cheese and a giant pitcher of Virgin Marys with Tabasco and celery sticks for garnish. You could smoke a pack of cigarettes or eat an entire sheet of crumb cake if you wanted and no one said a word. Most of the Johnsons are obese chain-smokers, and if, like me, you are not, and on top of that, never drank to excess, you are admired almost every day, from every angle. I am the Jackie Kennedy of the Johnson family and it's been a wonderful thing. We still go to Racine for the major holidays.

My brother went a different way, as casting directors like to say in Hollywood, which is where he settled and what he became. After twenty years of smoking pot every day, for his health, as he put it, Andy found himself at a dinner party in West Hollywood, seated next to a handsome tree surgeon in good, but not coke-fueled, spirits, with compatible politics, no diseases, and absolutely no interest in celebrities. According to Andy, who was calling me with updates from restaurant vestibules, men's clothing stores, and his own bathroom, they had amazing sex fourteen days in a row, without pot or liquor, at the end of which Andy said, Please, marry me, and Michael said, You bet, and they bought a house in Silver Lake the day it went on the market. Andy said that if Michael and affordable housing weren't signs of a Higher Power, he didn't know what were and he quit everything cold turkey the day they moved in, dropping off a four-hundred-dollar Moroccan hookah and a bunch of hand-blown glass bongs at the men's homeless shelter on the way. For the last eight years, he's been doing an hour of yoga every morning, much the way the Johnsons drink coffee, bake, and whittle. Aside from being in much better shape than he used to be, Andy is the same good and dear person he always was, although

Michael says, when I'm visiting, as I'm sure Jay says about me, it's not all sweetness and light. You will have noticed that neither of us has children.

I'd been waiting for the call about my father since he turned seventy. I thought that would be a nice gift from the universe—ten or fifteen healthy years of widowhood for my mother, traveling with friends, taking courses at the Elderhostel, and winding up in her eighties on a hotel veranda sipping a tall, fruity drink with someone who looked like Mr. Rachlin. I hoped Mr. Rachlin was still alive and I hoped that my father wouldn't dawdle in shuffling off this mortal coil. He'd had a fairly serious car accident when he was sixty-eight, which left him limping a little, and he was a heavy cigar smoker, which seemed promising. I sent him crystal ashtrays and silver cigar cutters for his birthdays, expensive humidors and a subscription to that stupid cigar magazine for Christmas, and when friends went to Cuba, I'd ask them to bring back a box for my father. I was, roughly speaking, watching the clock.

Their next-door neighbor found my name on the tiny phone list my mother kept taped to the kitchen wall. Your father's too upset, Mrs. Cannon said, so I'm calling. Andy and I met at the airport and rented a car and drove to our house. Mrs. Rachlin greeted us very warmly and Mr. Rachlin waited in the living room, sitting next to my father, who was reading the paper. Mr. Rachlin jumped up to hug us. He jerked his head toward my father. "It hasn't really sunk in," he said, and Andy and I nodded. My father said, "Hey, kids." Mrs. Cannon left a lasagna on the kitchen table. Broadway Delicatessen delivered platters twice, fried chicken from the hospital where my mother volunteered, and right before dinnertime, six pounds of corned beef and pastrami, with a pound each of cole slaw and kosher dills, from my father's law firm. We let the Rachlins go home and I gave Mr. Rachlin a little kiss for my mother's sake. My father unwrapped the corned beef and made himself a sandwich.

"You kids want some?"

We said we weren't hungry. My father ate his sandwich over the sink.

"You slimmed down," he said to Andy. "The trick is keeping it off. Discipline. Without that, the avoirdupois just piles back on."

I put all the food in the fridge and, for the same reason that I still recut the flowers in a bouquet before I put them in a vase with an aspirin and always put scented soaps in with my underwear and cedar chips in with my sweaters in May, that is, because I am my mother's daughter, I made us all sit down in the living room, To Talk.

"Go ahead," my father said, flirting with a corner of the front page.

"Daddy," is how I started, and I couldn't say another word. On the phone I always called him Alvin, as if it were a joke.

Andy picked up the ball and ran with it. Nope, my father said. No sitting shiva; your mother and I didn't believe in that. And no memorial service; your mother wouldn't have wanted that. I couldn't imagine why she wouldn't have wanted it but my father was adamant about everything. Cremation, he said; your mother felt very strongly about that—you know she hated cemeteries. And I'll take care of it.

"We'd like to participate," I said.

"The fact is," my father said, "I already had it taken care of."

"Where's the urn," I said.

My father laughed. "What, you don't believe me?" He pointed to the sideboard, and we saw a black box about the size of a lunch thermos and sealed with gold tape, sitting next to a bottle of Tia Maria, two bottles of sherry, and a bottle of Scotch someone gave my father fourteen years ago. Andy and I got up to look at it.

"And the will," my brother said. "I'm just asking because—

"She left everything to me," my father said, "but if you kids want something from her jewelry box, go ahead and take it."

My father picked up the paper in both hands, and we went into their bedroom, which was as neat as it always had been, except for my father's underwear on my mother's bargello bench. Her jewelry box was on their dresser, centered beneath their big Venetian mirror.

"I wish she had something you'd want," I said.

"She kept Poppa's watch in the bottom," he said. "I'll take that. I don't think the Erwin Pearl clip-ons are going to work for me."

Our grandfather's handsome old Hamilton watch was not in the bottom of her jewelry box. And her good pearls were gone and her diamond watch and the sapphire earrings and matching bracelet she'd bought for herself on her sixtieth birthday, cashing in the bonds her father left her.

"Daddy," I said. "Mom's good stuff is missing."

"Nothing's missing," he said coldly, and I thought, Christ, I'm going to have to show him, but he cleared his throat and said, "I put all of her valuables in a safety-deposit box. With people in and out of the house, it seemed smart."

There was no answer to that. "Oh, good thinking," I said. I went back to their bedroom with a handful of plastic bags.

"Just take half of it," I told Andy. "In case you have a daughter or you have a friend with a daughter or you start dressing up. Just take half of every fucking thing that's in there."

He picked up a turquoise bracelet and a handful of cheap Indian bangles and I nodded. I put the beautiful Italian shoes she stopped wearing when she got bunions into a garbage bag and I put the beautiful heavy silk French scarves that she wore until she died in my suitcase. When Andy and I had cleaned out her closet and her jewelry box, leaving her track suits and sneakers and her sensible poly-silk blouses for my father to deal with, we went into my room. I pressed the push lock on the door.

"Please sleep in here," I said.

Andy patted my hand. "We didn't say good night."

"Good night," we both yelled through the closed door.

"Good night, kids," he yelled back. "I'll be back for lunch."

We took a walk in the morning and threw some bad costume jewelry (Boca Bohemian, Oaxaca Farm Girl) into Long Island Sound and cried and talked while the gulls circled and we waited until my father came back. I made three corned-beef-pastrami-and-cole-slaw sandwiches and we each took an A&P diet soda from the case on the kitchen counter.

"So," Andy said. "No service, no interment, no obit, and no visiting. Is that it?"

"That's it," my father said.

"Do you need anything?" I said.

"Like what?" my father said.

"We'll head to the airport this afternoon, then," Andy said.

"Sure," my father said. "You've got jobs, don't you?"

I didn't stop speaking to my father. I did what my mother would have wanted me to do. (I like to think that her wish was for my father to have slipped painlessly and just hours after Andy was born into a deep crack in the world and never return, but I could never get her to say so. What I wanted was to have come out of her womb armed to my little baby lips and killed him with my superpowers before the cord was cut.) My weekly phone calls had none of my mother's social flourishes. (It doesn't hurt to be nice, she said, but that wasn't true in this case.) I did make sure my father wasn't dead and that he was not, with his driving, a danger to others or, with some old-man slippage in hygiene or nutrition, a danger to himself. I hired Delphine Jones to keep the house tidy and to look in on him three times a week, and when she couldn't stand him anymore ("Your father is a very exacting man," she said, her island lilt just about knocked flat after days and weeks with Alvin Lowald), she would pass him on to a colleague for a week of R & R.

Delphine called me on a Wednesday afternoon in January.

"I see the pipes have burst," she said. "Your father isn't sure who to call."

I called Andy, and he called a plumber, who, for only fourteen hundred dollars up front, would make things right, and I found the Cutler Brothers Catastrophe Company, whose receptionist said, very kindly, that they specialized in "this kind of thing," and I canceled my appointments and got back on a plane to make sure that things were okay. ("I'll give you a million dollars if I don't have to go this time" Andy said. "Seriously. I will give you a weekend at the spa of your choice. I will buy you diamond earrings.")

I rang the doorbell and my father let me in. Aside from needing a haircut, he looked good. The house did not. And it smelled the way it had forty years ago, when our whole family sat on the kitchen porch and watched Long Island Sound rise past the pear tree and onto the driveway and then into the TV room, which had never really recovered.

"Better late than never," he said. "The girl left a note for you."

The note said, as I knew it would, that Delphine found herself too busy to clean for my father, and it was her distinct impression that he actually needed more than a cleaning person since, as she wrote in her neat, curvy handwriting, there was an exceptional amount of filth and personal uncleanliness accumulating from week to week (she itemized the most offensive occurrences at the bottom of the page). She was happy to recommend Beate Jaszulski, a Polish person who had been a nurse in Poland and whom she had met at adult education. She left me Beate's number. My father and I ate the only things in the refrigerator, hard-boiled eggs and American cheese, and he asked why Andy hadn't come. I said Andy was very busy, and my father snorted.

"Busy sucking some guy's cock," my father said.

"You know," I said conversationally, "we try to be nice to you.

We try to be nice, which isn't easy because you are an emotional black hole and the coldest, most self-centered sonofabitch I have ever known, we try to be nice in honor of our mother's memory. So, if you can't be civil, why don't you just shut the fuck up?"

My father took his slice of cheese into the living room and read until he heard me go to bed.

In the morning, I showered with my mother's Arpège bath soap and used her antique hair dryer and got dressed and started again. I suggested that it might be wise to sell the house and move into assisted living. Near me, I even said.

"The only way I'm leaving this house is feetfirst," he said.

I have to say, I did laugh and I did say, "That's not a problem." Oh, we should have smothered him the night after my mother died, we should have just snuck into their bedroom, pulled back that Venetian damask duvet cover she was so proud of, put the matching pillows over his face, and leaned in until he stopped moving.

"Look," I said, "You can sell the house and move into assisted living or you can keep the house and hire someone to care for you—a housekeeper-type person—and you do that for as long as you can afford it, and then your backup plan is you die before you run out of money."

"Fine," my father said. "Hire someone. A nice pair of tits wouldn't hurt."

Beate Jaszulski moved into my old room. My father handed her the car keys. (What do I need the hassle for? People drive like god-damn idiots around here anyway.) And every Friday, she dropped him off at the five o'clock movie, while she did the grocery shopping. She kept the house clean, he said (You can eat off the god-damn floor) and cooked the meals he preferred (Just plain food, he said, no French song and dance). Two boiled eggs and dry rye toast every morning, a grilled cheese sandwich every day for lunch, and two broiled lamb chops and rice for dinner, or sometimes, caution to the winds, she cooked a small rib eye with a side of mashed potatoes. I know this because I spoke to Beate every Sunday and she would recite the meals cooked, the walks taken, the minor household repairs her cousin Janek performed and she billed us for. She never complained about my father and she never criticized me for not visiting. At the end of every conversation, I'd ask to speak with my father, and she'd say, "Sure. Sure, you want to talk to Dad," sympathetically, as if she understood that I was so eager to talk to him, I just couldn't stand another moment of chitchat.

"Alvin," I said.

"Alison."

"How's it going?"

"Can't complain."

"Okay. Good. Everything good with Beate?" What did I think? She would rob him and he would know and report it to me, in due time? She would, at not quite five feet tall and as big around, and sixty-five if she was a day, hurt him or seduce him?

"It's okay." Sometimes he would tell me that Beate listened to the radio too loud or used too much ammonia on the kitchen floor or he'd found the lamb a little tough, and I would mention these things to her very delicately and she'd say, "I take care of it." No complaint was ever repeated. Andy referred to her as Mother Beate and he made a lot of jokes about the number of old men she had buried and their grateful children. ("That's how she got that Porsche and that house in Cap-Ferrat," he said. "God bless her.")

After about a year with Beate:

"Alvin," I said.

"Alison. Alibaloo."

"Dad? Are you all right?"

"Never better. Bea—how am I?"

I heard Beate talking in the background and my father chuckled and he said, "There you go. I'm—how old am I, Bea?—there you go, I'm eighty-eight and holding my own. No pun intended."

Beate got on the phone and told me that her own mother was dying in Poland and she had to fly home.

"Just for a week. I be back for Mr. Lovald. I go on a Saturday, I be back on a Sunday."

I asked if Beate had any thoughts about who would keep my father company, make his meals, drive him on his errands, do his laundry. "Forget the laundry," I said. "It can pile up for a week. Who will do the other things," I asked Beate, and there was a long, flat Polish silence.

"Fine," I said. "I'll be there Saturday and we can do the . . . handoff."

Beate understood well enough what I meant and her voice brightened as we went back to her plans, which included dry-cleaning her raincoat, buying a pair of good boots, laying in a supply of frozen lamb chops and clean boxers for my father for a week, and bringing peanut butter to Ruda Slaska.

"Janek will take me to airport," she said. "Newark."

My cab pulled up in front of the house at four o'clock. Beate showed me the eggs, the sliced American cheese, the rye bread, and the fourteen frozen lamb chops. She handed me the keys. She gestured toward my parents' bedroom.

"He naps," she said. "I see him Sunday. Seven days." She held up seven fingers and then she picked up her suitcase and waved good-bye. As she stepped onto the porch, a car appeared, and my guess was that her cousin had parked up the street and was just waiting for my cab to leave.

Beate was out the door, and it would be just me and Alvin for the next seven days, unless I killed him, in which case I would spend at least half the week in jail. The house looked, somehow, more like my childhood home than it had for the last twenty years. Beate had found my mother's old spring slipcovers and covered the cigar-burned navy couch with pink and yellow chintz and she'd even found the yellow chintz pillows and the yellow-and-white-striped slipcover that went on my father's armchair. It was all aggressively and hopelessly cheerful, and I expected my mother to walk out of the kitchen, wiping her hands on a clean apron, and saying either, "Who wants quiche?" which was a good day or, "There's no reason to upset him," which was not.

"Bea? Bea?" My father was yelling, pretty loudly.

I opened the door a crack. I had no wish to be in my parents' bedroom with my father, where he still slept on his side of the bed and where there was still, on my mother's nightstand, a box of tissues and a paperback.

"It's me, Dad. It's Alison. Beate'll be back in a week. I'm here in the meantime."

"What?" he said and he sat up, patting his nightstand all over for his glasses, which were lying on the floor. I handed him his glasses.

"Thank you. You're a good kid," he said.

His hair was going in four different directions and there were little scabs on his chest and the backs of his hands. He scratched a scab until it bled and he pressed his bleeding wrist against the sheet.

"Where's Bea?"

"She's gone to see her mother. In Poland. Her mother's not well," I said, and I was trying not to yell because I knew that yelling did not help people understand you better.

"That's a shame," he said. "My mother died when I was nineteen and my father, I don't think he got over it. He became an old man overnight. You know what I mean?" I did know what he meant, of course, but since I had never heard my father mention his mother or his father or the emotional state of any living being, I was speechless.

"An old man overnight, Alison," he said.

"I know what you mean," I said. "You want some lunch?"

I made two grilled cheese sandwiches and I wondered whether I should offer my father a beer, since on one hand, I had no idea who he was and in his altered state, alcohol might be bad for him, and on the other hand, what the hell. My father and I had our sandwiches. ("Burn it," he said. "That's what they used to say in the diner. Put a farmer on the raft and burn it." "What diner?" I said, and my father said, not unkindly, "Well, you're no Julia Child.") And we drank our beers.

"Salud, amor, y dinero," he said and clinked my bottle. "Is everybody okay?"

"Sure," I said. I didn't know who everybody was. He called Andy Fatso, he called Michael The Faigele, he called Jay Babe, the Blue Ox, and my mother had been dead for two years.

"I'll take a grilled cheese sandwich," he said.

"Another? Okay." Was this good? It could be good, an appetite for life or something like that, or it could be that he didn't know if he'd eaten or not.

"Can't I get some lunch?" he said, and I made the sandwich, which he nibbled and then he said, "I'm gonna take a little nap." He stood up and waited for me to stand up.

I walked him to the bedroom and to his bed and he used my arm to swing himself into bed.

"Good kid," he said, patting my face.

I called Jay and he said, "You are too Julia Child," and we exchanged I love yous and he said, "Hurry home," and I said I would.

I called my brother and told him that he might not want to miss the Second Coming of Alvin Lowald, in which our father had been snatched by pod people who'd sent us a nice old man who thanked me and called me a good kid.

"Is this permanent?" Andy asked.

"I don't know. Maybe he'll be back to normal tomorrow."

"Great. Back to the crypt. Does it *seem* like he's dying—is this pre-death niceness?"

I swore to him that our father did not seem to be dying, that he had done a good job on one and a half grilled cheese sandwiches and all of a Heineken and was now snoring loudly in his bed. Andy swore back that he would get on the redeye Thursday night, as soon as they were done casting a police drama in which none of the criminals or women could be more than five feet five, which was the height of this particular TV detective.

"Does he know you?" Andy said.

"I don't know. He looks glad to see me, so no. But he called me Alison, so yes."

"See you Friday, unless he completely recovers, in which case you won't see me at all."

"You better get me those earrings," I said, and we hung up. I read my father's magazines until I fell asleep.

In my dream, it is pouring rain and I am driving our old Dodge Dart. My father's standing patiently on the steps of the old library, without a coat or an umbrella. He gets into the car and I have to help him with his seat belt. He clasps his wet hands in his lap. I want to drive him to his new apartment in the assisted living place, but he doesn't know the address and neither do I.

I'll just pop out here for directions, Daddy, I say, hoping that the two women I see standing under the green awning of a pretty restaurant will be knowledgeable and helpful and guide us to the assisted living place. They're not and they don't. One of the women says, Is that your father in the car? And I say, yes, that's why we're looking for his apartment, and she says she certainly never drove her father all over kingdom come in a goddamned monsoon without even an address, and the other one says, What a harebrained scheme, and they sound, together, exactly like my father, as I've known him. I get back into the car and my father looks at me with hope and just a little anxiety.

Is everybody okay? he says.

Yes, we are, I say, and I just start driving in the pouring rain, hoping that one of us will see something familiar.

My father yelled, "Bea, Bea," and I woke up and ran down the hall. I turned on the overhead light and handed my father his glasses as I sat down on the edge of the bed.

"Oh," he said, and he clutched my hand. Any fool could see that he knew it was me. "You're here."

"I'm here. You probably had a bad dream," I said.

"Could be." He'd already lost interest. "That's a pretty necklace," he said. "Was it your mother's?"

"No. I don't have any of Mom's jewelry."

"That's a shame," he said. "I would think you'd have kept a few of her things, to remind you."

I nodded.

"Well, we were a lucky family," he said. "All around us those years, kids were doing drugs, getting in trouble. People were divorcing, right and left. I always used to say, you know, at parties or things, 'This is my original wife.' We were lucky."

I nodded again and took such a deep breath I felt my ribs separating from my sternum.

My father lay back down and I patted his hand. I smoothed the sheet.

"I'm going to turn out the light. I'll see you in the morning."

I got to the door and turned off the light.

My father said, "Is everybody okay?"

PERMAFROST

Terrible is terrible, Frances thought. There's no comparing one bad thing to another. Whatever it is—hands blown off in Angolan minefields, children in Chernobyl with tumors like softballs, a car accident right around the corner—there's no measuring suffering. Mrs. Shenker disagreed. At night, while her daughter, Beth, was knocked out by morphine, Mrs. Shenker sat in the solarium, the waiting room for the adolescent-medicine unit. She sat back in a recliner and read aloud from her stack of printouts about the flesh-eating bacteria that had attacked Beth nine days ago.

"Listen to this one," she said to Frances. "And hold on to your hat. 'I was diagnosed with necrotizing fasciitis after a vacation in the Bahamas. We still don't know what caused it. Even though I've had approximately thirty-four operations and three skin grafts on my legs and groin and continue to have some trouble with my lungs and kidneys, I consider myself lucky. My wife and I have run into some financial difficulties and I am unable to drive but we count our blessings every day.' Can you fucking believe this? Well, you probably can—you're a social worker."

Frances could believe it. Frances's father raised Frances and her sister, Sherri, on stories of polar expeditions that began with terrible errors in judgment and ended with men weeping over frozen corpses, with people suffering horribly and still thanking God for not having killed them outright when they got on the ship. When Sherri was eighteen and Frances was eleven, Sherri said, "I want to experience Jesus' love and I want to help other young people know that they are not doomed." "Doomed to what?" Mr. Cairn had said, but he said it to the front hall because Sherri had already run out the door, and it was no different, really, than a girl going off to be a Deadhead or driving to Los Angeles with some badass to become a porn star. When people in the neighborhood asked where Sherri was, Mr. Cairn said, "We lost her," and nobody pressed him and they certainly didn't know he meant she'd gone to join the Exodus Ministry in Indianapolis. Sherri sent a Christmas card every year, and other than that, it was just Frances and her father, the storyteller.

S.S. *TERRA NOVA*

"*This* one's a day brightener," Mrs. Shenker said. "This guy's an amputee himself, and a world-class athlete . . ." Mrs. Shenker skimmed ahead a few lines. "Well, not a world-class athlete, clearly. But athletic, and he's invented these special responsive feet that give energy back to the leg, so you don't just walk around, clump, clump, clump, and there's a special suction cup so the whole leg just goes on—" She makes a sharp, sucking sound.

Mr. Shenker stood up. "I'm going to take a little walk," he said. Mrs. Shenker and Frances saw him through the glass block wall of the solarium, chatting with Theresa the charge nurse and, like magic, two more nurses showed up and they passed a box of doughnuts around and Theresa disappeared for a moment and then reappeared, carrying real coffee cups and giving one to Mr. Shenker. Mrs. Shenker had the solarium and the doctors and Mr. Shenker had the nurses. Frances had bumped into him a couple of times when he was walking out of an empty exam room, straightening his tie, and when she looked over her shoulder, she saw a nurse come out and lock the door behind her. The nurses looked transformed; they looked as if they had been handed something immensely valuable and fragile, whose care could not be entrusted to ordinary women. Mr. Shenker looked as he always did, handsome and doomed.

Frances said to Mrs. Shenker, "I have a few patients to check on. Do you want to sit with Beth?"

"Isn't she napping?"

Frances admitted that Beth probably was napping. (Although napping was not the right word; Beth Shenker was on enough methadone to anesthetize a three-hundred-pound man and the only thing that woke her for the first eight days was a gnawing pain of the kind you get with pancreatic cancer. On the bright side, while almost no one survives pancreatic cancer, Frances thought that Beth Shenker, like most necrotizing-fasciitis victims, would survive into old age.)

Mrs. Shenker said, "All right, it's almost time for *Judge Judy*. I'll go watch that with Beth. Tell Mr. Shenker where I am, when you see him."

Beth was dreaming. She was five, jumping up and down on her new big-girl bed in the middle of the night, clean sheets under her soft, pretty feet, the cool air tickling her soles as she jumped higher and higher, and in the dream, her little feet lit up the dark room like fireflies.

Lorraine Shenker smoothed Beth's sheet over the metal hoop that protected her legs and straightened out Beth's IV line and kept her eyes on Judge Judy, who was looking over her bifocals to tell a fat nineteen-year-old African American mother of twins that she *deserved* to lose custody of her children. The way Judge Judy waved her hand dismissively and then slipped off the bifocals to award damages to the girl's attractive, well-dressed brother, whose car the young mother had totaled while he looked after those twins, was wonderful. It would be nice if there were a *Dr.* Judy, handing down diagnoses and reversing the decisions of other, dumber doctors. Dr. Judy would have taken one look at Beth and said, firmly, This young lady is not going to have a gross and permanent disability. Case dismissed.

Frances walked past Beth's room, reading over Beth's chart, and by the time she got to the nurses' desk, Nathan Silverman was taking the cruller she wanted. Nathan Silverman was Beth's surgeon, and he'd done a great job and he told everyone he'd done a great job, and Frances thought, Narcissistic grandiosity with excellent fine-motor skills, and thinking that made her smile warmly whenever she ran into him.

Dr. Silverman smiled back, yellow pieces of cruller flying everywhere, and Frances said, "Hey, Dr. Silverman," and put her hand on her second choice, a chocolate doughnut. Her fingers sank deep into the chocolate icing. Dr. Silverman brushed the crumbs from his tie and stretched his arms over his head. Finally, he said, "Is Maria Lopez around?"

Frances said, "I'm not sure. Maybe it's her break," and she picked up a napkin with her free hand.

She didn't say, If you get a move on, you can probably catch up with Maria Lopez when she comes out of Exam Room #2, right after Mr. Shenker.

"I just thought Maria might be chatting with Beth," Dr. Silverman said. "You know, cheering her up."

"Could be," Frances said.

Maria Lopez was the pinup girl of the adolescent-medicine unit. She liked to slip off her white clogs and massage her lovely calves at the end of her shift and give everyone a good look at her rhinestone-studded toe ring.

What kind of grown woman wears a toe ring? Frances thought.

Dr. Silverman said only, "Let's get Beth thinking about recovery. She's just a kid, Frances."

Frances thought about Beth's recovery all the time. Beth was thirteen, and although she could wear long sleeves to hide the river of scars that would always run up her right forearm and she could wear turtlenecks to hide the thick red web spread across her collarbone, she would always have a stump at the end of her left leg, and if Frances Cairn had had to contemplate all that at thirteen, she's pretty sure she would have flipped open her laptop as soon as she was conscious and Googled the most effective form of suicide.

S.S. *ENDURANCE*

Dear Beth,

I hope your recovery is continuing to progress. As I hope you know, everyone at the hospital was impressed with your fortitude.

Frances crossed out "fortitude" and wrote "strength of character" and went back to "fortitude," which sounded sort of magnificent, even if Beth was unlikely to know what *fortitude* meant. Frances had never seen Beth read anything. Frances was with her every day for almost a month, holding her hands while Beth screamed as her arms and legs were debrided and bringing endless cups of juice and endless bags of ice chips. Frances watched Beth come out of two comas, and each time, she was the person who comforted Beth after Mrs. Shenker and Dr. Silverman had to tell Beth what day it was and how long her coma had lasted and then finally told Beth that she had only one foot. Frances did everything she could to bond with Beth and the Shenker family; at Beth's discharge, she walked the Shenkers to the lobby, she gave Beth a care package from the staff (lip balm and Lifesavers, a photo of Beth and the floor staff, a pink T-shirt that said NO LIMITS!, and a little stuffed penguin with a red-and-white Red Cross scarf around its neck). Between the multiple surgeries and the painkillers and the life ahead, Beth was hardly speaking when she left, and when Frances promised to visit Beth at home, Beth nodded, with her eyes closed, and the Shenkers drove off.

Dear Beth,

I've been meaning to visit for the past three weeks but things have been really hectic at the hospital. Remember your old room 13a, the nicest private room? A new patient is in there. T—— has two broken legs—nothing compared to you, I know—and sadly, his father is facing charges for having thrown him off the roof of their apartment building. T——'s mother doesn't speak English and we have not yet found an Eritrean interpreter but Dr. Silverman—I know you remember him—seems to think that if I act out each of his phrases carefully, T——'s mother will understand what's going on. . . .

Frances's handwriting hadn't changed since the sixth grade. It was the round, hopeful handwriting of girls who wrote things like: *So glad we sat together in Econ! You rock. Let's B BFF. You are so awesome. Don't ever stop being who U R!* over the pictures of CLASS CUT-UPS and the YOUTH EFFECTIVENESS SEMINAR; things that she, Frances, had never actually written to anyone. Frances's friends were the disfigured and the disabled, one way or another, and Beth Shenker would have been one of the pretty, giggling girls who looked right through them as they limped and staggered down the hall.

Dear Beth,

I've spoken to your parents several times and told them of my plan to visit you. They couldn't care less, so I am coming this Saturday morning, with cider and doughnuts. Just like old times . . .

Kentucky Fried Chicken. ("Terrible stuff," Mr. Cairn said. "Awful," Frances said, and she passed the cole slaw and the biscuits they loved, a triple order every time, and the creamed spinach. It was a relief to eat hot food that neither of them had to cook, and they had done this every Friday night since Frances moved out to go to social-work school.)

"I'm raking tomorrow," Mr. Cairn said. "Want to help out your old man?"

"I can't. I'm following up with a patient. The girl who contracted necrotizing fasciitis."

Mr. Cairn loved to hear about the dreadful things that befell Frances's people and to hear about the things that she did to help them bear their various crosses. He might have gone into social work himself, instead of hardware, if anyone had encouraged him. Mr. Cairn shook his head sympathetically. "I can't imagine." He finished his second biscuit. "The one with one foot and the father who's a ladies' man?" and Frances nodded. One night, instead of going back to her apartment after work, she'd driven over to watch *Law & Order* with her father, and she told him all about flesh-eating bacteria and the Shenkers.

"Is this an all-day visit?" Mr. Cairn said. "Because I don't like the sound of this household."

"I won't be there for more than an hour."

Mr. Cairn pushed his chicken around on his plate.

"I could drive you," he said.

"Daddy, you have to get a life." Frances smiled when she said it.

Mr. Cairn put his fork and knife on his plate and he took Frances's hand.

"There's someone special I'd like you to meet," he said.

When Frances's mother died, her father staggered from room to room, crying. Frances and Sherri would walk into the garage for their bikes and find their father sprawled on the hood of the car, face buried in his chamois cloths. One Sunday morning, Sherri dumped a basket of wet clothes in the middle of the living room. "I can't do it," she said. "I mean, I actually cannot do laundry. Daddy's crying in front of the dryer."

The first day of first grade, Frances had to walk next door and ask Mrs. Cohen to fix her hair because her father was crying so hard, he couldn't do her braids. Mrs. Cohen did them and did them again the next day, and on the third day Mr. Cairn took Frances to the barber and said, Please give her a haircut. Something short. And pretty.

If he had married Mrs. Cohen he would not now be sitting in front of her with a crumb of fried chicken on his face, telling her to get ready to meet someone special.

"Sure," Frances said.

"Maybe she'll take me off your hands," Mr. Cairn said.

S.S. *ENDEAVOR*

A short, wide woman with Mrs. Shenker's sharp chin and thick eyebrows opened the door.

"I am—" Frances said, trying to hold on to her muffler and her purse and the bag of doughnuts and the jug of cider and the brochure about a camp for teenagers with physical limitations, and Mr. Shenker came into the front hall and opened the door wider.

"Hey. This is Miss . . . Frances," he said. "Sylvia, this is Frances. Frances, my mother-in-law, Sylvia Winik. Frances spent time with Beth at the hospital. Jesus, Frances, you look like Shackleton on his way to the North Pole."

"I doubt it," Frances said. Frances was *raised* on Ernest Shackleton and brave Robert Edwin Peary and that moron Robert Scott and the tragedy of his ponies, eaten by the explorers, because Captain Scott was too stupid to use a dog team. ("Too much an admirer of dogs, the way Englishmen sometimes are," her father had said, as if they both knew people like that, people who loved their dogs so much they would try to go to the South Pole with horses, to spare the dogs discomfort.) Frances knew the beginnings and ends of every polar expedition and nothing she ever did was going to be like Ernest Shackleton, who was a hero in her household, like Kennedy or King, and Mr. Shenker could just keep his big, fat, condescending, adulterous mouth closed.

"You might be thinking of Lawrence Oates," Frances said, and Mr. Shenker looked at his mother-in-law and smiled. Lawrence Oates was one of the youngest men to accompany Scott and also the smartest, and when he understood he was dying of starvation and frostbite, he stopped eating entirely, gave away his compass, and lifted the flap of his tent to walk into the snow. "I am going outside now," he said, "and I may be some time." In their game of Great Expedition, this had been Frances's favorite part, and she would say those lines and run onto the porch, in her pajamas, and her father would wait just the right amount of time and then carry her back in, as if there were icicles hanging all over her and she had just hours to live.

"Lorraine," Mr. Shenker called out. "Frances is here. From the hospital."

Mrs. Shenker came down the hall in sweatpants and a T-shirt, her hair in a ponytail.

"Frances, aren't you sweet," she said. "I didn't know you were . . . Well, how nice. I was just doing some laundry. I thought it was going to rain, so we gave up on golf." She put her hand on Mr. Shenker's chest and he put an arm around her waist. "You were right, I was wrong," she said.

"We'll golf tomorrow," he said. "Sylvia can spoil Beth and we'll steal away." The Shenkers and Mrs. Shenker's mother all smiled at one another and finally Mrs. Shenker said, "Well, thank you for bringing a treat for Beth. Although, my God, we all ate enough doughnuts at that hospital . . ."

Mr. Shenker said, "Always room for a few more."

Mrs. Shenker said, "Let's just take a peek at Miss Beth and see how she's doing."

"Hey, Frances," Beth said. Beth was smiling and she wore a silky green T-shirt over her bandages and a green headband. There was a pull-up bar above her head and her bedroom was decorated like a tropical paradise. She sat in the middle of her big green-and-blue bed, surrounded by her laptop, her iPhone, and her remote control. A flat-screen TV was mounted on the opposite wall, with white-capped waves painted to unfurl around it. The doorway was as wide as a hospital room's. Pale-green mermaids raised their arms on either side of it, and there was an old-fashioned map of the world's oceans painted on the wood floor, and a wheelchair was folded up in one corner.

Mrs. Shenker saw Frances looking. "I know—we went all out. We had an architect in here and Beth drove him crazy until everything was just the way she wanted."

Beth grinned and looked down to text someone.

"Pretty cool, right? I might become an architect. The disabled Americans thing, plus I love design. Did you see my dresser?" Her dresser was painted to look like a treasure chest, with gold coins and jewels glued all the way down the front, as if the treasure were spilling out. "That was my idea."

Frances sat in the small, comfortable armchair and Beth chatted a little, and answered e-mail. (Oh, my God, she said. No way. *No* way.) She texted friends and smiled at Frances to show that she didn't mean to be rude and went back to her laptop. Mrs. Shenker's mother came in with a plate of peanut-butter-and-fluff sandwiches, each half topped with a strawberry slice and two glasses of milk.

"Nana, thank you," Beth said, and her grandmother kissed her and said, "Physical therapy in an hour, young lady," and Beth struck a strongman pose and then offered Frances a sandwich and a napkin. Beth played some music on her computer and Frances and Beth ate their sandwiches, as if they were two girls in seventh grade, taking a homework break.

Frances ate her sandwich halves and thanked Mrs. Shenker's mother, who handed her a couple of warm cookies for the road. The Shenkers emerged arm in arm to thank Frances for coming. They told her that Beth was starting school in three weeks, and Mr. Shenker said, She's nervous about it, but you know Beth—she always gets back on the horse.

Frances got in her car and drove around the corner and pulled over, to just sit for a while.

S.S. *DISCOVERY*

Dear Beth,

I saw your picture today. Everyone in America must have seen it, plastered on the cover of People *magazine. You look wonderful. Everything that was just on the cusp in you, when I knew you ten years ago, has absolutely flowered. I was sorry to read that your grandmother had passed but your parents look very well and, of course, very proud. I'm sure you are an inspiration to everyone around you, just as they said in the magazine. To have done what you've done—the Paralympics and now the triathlon and your work with teenagers—is very impressive.*

Things have been quieter, here. I'm actually still at the hospital. I'm the Assistant Director of Social Work, which sounds like more than it is. I handle the scheduling and the outpatient programs but I don't do any hiring or firing.

My father—I think you met him the time my car broke down at your house—passed away about five years ago. I miss him. It's weird, at least it's weird to me, but I now spend most Friday nights with his widow, Carol Skolnick. I don't know if I ever mentioned it (probably not—we didn't really talk about me, which was appropriate, since my home visits were for you and to help with your post-traumatic recovery), but my father remarried during the time you and I were in contact. Anyway, Carol and I weren't exactly close when my father was alive but since he died, she's reached out to me, and now on Friday nights she lights a Yarsight candle (I don't know if I've spelled this correctly) for my father and for all of the other people we know who have died (I don't include patients; we just mourn the people we've known in our personal lives) and then we have dinner, which is usually Kentucky Fried Chicken. It's sort of a tradition.

The other big change is that I am in touch with my sister, Sherri, who was not part of my life when you and I knew each other. Sherri lives in Indianapolis and she and her husband run a cleaning service. They clean up after storms and other natural disasters in people's offices and homes and also just regular cleaning. They have two girls, who are almost as old as you were when I met you, and they are wonderful girls. I only wish I had known them sooner. Sherri called me after our father died and she said to me, Your only family is me, and I remember saying that it didn't seem like she wanted me in her life and she said that that wasn't true, that our father had just abandoned her after her religious experience (my sister is, I guess, a born-again Christian and my father and I were the kind of Congregationalists who didn't bother anyone, and I guess that was an insurmountable difference between them, plus my father and I thought Sherri was gay, which bothered her more than us but she stopped being gay, apparently, when she became born again and married Paul and had the girls). It's a little odd being in their house sometimes, with Jesus on every wall and pillow and Sherri censors the girls' reading, like no Harry Potter because of the magic. (I have to say this doesn't make any sense to me. What makes magic particularly anti-Christian? I understand that calling up Satan is definitely not good but I can't see how Tinkerbell or flying carpets threaten anyone.) But it is their house and their rules, and my nieces are happy and loving girls, and Paul has been very welcoming in his quiet way, and I am really grateful to spend their birthdays and Christmas with Sherri and her family.

I've continued my interest in polar exploration and the great expeditions, although I think it's safe to say this is not a subject of general interest. They were just so phenomenally brave. They lived on dog meat and willow tea. They boiled old boots and ate them. They ate the deerskin ties off their tents and then they cut up their tents to make footgear, so they could go out and look for the rescue ships. Lieutenant George DeLong of the U.S. Navy spent two winters frozen in place 750 miles from the North Pole, which is not that far—others had traveled farther—and then his ship sank on June 12, 1881. There were fourteen of them left, and still he wrote in his journal, "All hands weak and feeble, but cheerful."

All my life, those men were my heroes. I think I would have been better off with the astronauts or even the Argonauts or with the saints, if we had been that kind of family, or with the people who marched on Selma for their rights. But my father loved these men and he didn't seem to notice that they were all, really, pretty crazy and most of them failures (Roald Amundsen was often the villain of these stories and I think now it was because he knew what he was doing; he accomplished his goal and he went on to other successes, and all of that was despicable to my father). These people made terrible mistakes and the best and worst of them just shrugged and said that it was no one's fault at all, just the nature of life, just the inevitable outcome of what they had undertaken, but it wasn't true. They had something missing. They left things behind that other, more reasonable men would have known to bring. They brought the wrong food, and the wrong transportation. They held the fucking maps upside down half the time and one boat fell to pieces in the Arctic Ocean because, when the ship had sailed in sunnier climes, the crew had pulled nails out of it to trade for sex with the Polynesian women, since iron was so valuable. They could have been saved by vitamins, which were easy to buy and carry. They could have been saved by a wireless transmitter, which was not uncommon.

On one of Peary's expeditions, their boat was struck by moving ice, pressed between two icebergs by the current, and as the ship was sinking, water coming in through the port side, the crew and the scientists gathered a few things and scrambled onto the icy bluff. Finn Hamilton went below three times, because he couldn't decide what to take. He brought a compass and threw it to a crewmate already on land. He went down for his pipe, and halfway up the stairs, he went back down again for his Bible and he slipped and drowned, tangled up with a footstool.

Some of us are Finn Hamilton and some of us are Beth Shenker, I guess. I have somehow not had the right things for this journey and I have packed and repacked a hundred times as if somehow the right thing will be found in some small pocket, put in by someone with more sense or gift than me, but I'm always scrambling for the last-minute thing and I am always, always watching the boat pull away without me.

Your family was one of my early boats and you were the bright and amazing sail, and I am, as I said at the beginning, very, very proud of you.

SLEEPWALKING

I was born smart and had been lucky my whole life, so I didn't even know that what I thought was careful planning was nothing more than being in the right place at the right time, missing an avalanche I didn't even hear.

After the funeral was over and the cold turkey and the glazed ham were demolished and some very good jazz was played and some very good musicians went home drunk on bourbon poured in my husband's honor, it was just me, my mother-in-law, Ruth, and our two boys, Lionel junior from Lionel's second marriage, and our little boy, Buster.

Ruth pushed herself up out of the couch, her black taffeta dress rustling reproachfully. I couldn't stand for her to start the dishes, sighing, praising the Lord, clucking her tongue over the state of my kitchen, in which the windows are not washed regularly and I do not scrub behind the refrigerator.

"Ruth, let them sit. I'll do them later tonight."

"No need to put off 'til tomorrow what we can do today. I'll do them right now, and then Lionel junior can run me home." Ruth does not believe that the good Lord intended ladies to drive;

she'd drive, eyes closed, with her drunk son or her accident-prone grandson before she'd set foot in my car.

"Ruth, please," I said. "I'd just as soon have something to do later. Please. Let me make us a cup of tea, and then we'll take you home."

Tea, her grandson Buster, and her son's relative sobriety were the three major contributions I'd made to Ruth's life; the tea and Buster accounted for all of our truces and the few good times we'd had together.

"I ought to be going along now, let you get on with things."

"Earl Grey? Darjeeling? Constant Comment? I've got some rosehip tea in here, too—it's light, sort of lemony." I don't know why I was urging her to stay; I'd never be rid of her as long as I had the boys. If Ruth no longer thought I was trash, she certainly made it clear that I hadn't lived up to her notion of the perfect daughter-in-law, a cross between Marian Anderson and Florence Nightingale.

"You have Earl Grey?" Ruth was wavering, half a smile on her sad mouth, her going-to-church lipstick faded to a blurry pink line on her upper lip.

When I really needed Ruth on my side, I'd set out an English tea: Spode teapot, linen place mats, scones, and three kinds of jam. And for half an hour, we'd sip and chew, happy to be so civilized.

"Earl Grey it is." I got up to put on the water, stepping on Buster, who was sitting on the floor by my chair, practically on my feet.

"Jesus, Buster, are you all right?" I hugged him before he could start crying and lifted him out of my way.

"The Lord's name," Ruth murmured, rolling her eyes up to apologize to Jesus personally. I felt like smacking her one, right in her soft dark face, and pointing out that since the Lord had not treated us especially well in the last year, during which we had both lost husbands, perhaps we didn't have to be overly concerned with His hurt feelings. Ruth made me want to be very, very bad.

"Sorry, Ruth. Buster, sit down by your grandmother, honey, and I'll make us all some tea."

"No, really, don't trouble yourself, Julia. Lionel junior, please take me home. Gabriel, come kiss your grandma good-bye. You boys be good, now, and think of how your daddy would want you to act. I'll see you all for dinner tomorrow."

She was determined to leave, martyred and tea-less, so I got in line to kiss her. Ruth put her hands on my shoulders, her only gesture of affection toward me, which also allowed her to pretend that she was a little taller, rather than a little shorter, than I am.

She left with Lionel junior, and Buster and I cuddled on the couch, his full face squashed against my chest, my skin resting on his soft hair. I felt almost whole.

"Sing, Mama."

Lionel had always wanted me to record with him and I had always said no, because I don't like performing and I didn't want to be a blues-singing Marion Davies to Lionel's William Randolph Hearst. But I loved to sing and he loved to play and I'm sorry we didn't record just one song together.

I was trying to think of something that would soothe Buster but not break my heart.

I sang "Amazing Grace," even though I can't quite hit that note, and I sang bits and pieces of a few more songs, and then Buster was asleep and practically drowning in my tears.

I heard Lionel junior's footsteps and blotted my face on my sleeve.

"Hey, Lion, let's put this little boy to bed."

"He's out, huh? You look tired, too. Why don't you go to bed and I'll do the dishes?"

That's my Lion. I think because I chose to love him, chose to be a mother and not just his father's wife, Lion gave me back everything he could. He was my table setter, car washer, garden weeder; in twelve years, I might've raised my voice to him twice. When my husband brought his son to meet me the first time, I looked into those wary eyes, hope pouring out of them despite himself, and I knew that I had found someone else to love.

I carried Buster to his room and laid him on the bed, slipping off his loafers. I pulled up the comforter with the long-legged basketball players running all over it and kissed his damp little face. I thought about how lucky I was to have Buster and Lion and even Ruth, who might torture me forever but would never abandon me, and I thought about how cold and lonely my poor Lionel must be, with no bourbon and no music and no audience, and I went into the bathroom to dry my face again. Lion got frantic when he saw me crying.

He was lying on the couch, his shoes off, his face turned toward the cushions.

"Want a soda or a beer? Maybe some music?" I pulled at his shoulder.

"Nope. Maybe some music, but not Pop's."

"No, no, not your father's. How about Billie Holiday, Sarah Vaughan?"

"How about something a little more up? How about Luther Vandross?" Lion turned around to face me.

"I don't have any—as you know." Lionel and I both hated bubblegum music, so of course Lion had the world's largest collection of whipped-cream soul; if it was insipid, he bought it.

"I'll get my tapes," he said, and sat halfway up to see if I would let him. We used to make him play them in his room so we wouldn't have to listen, but Lionel wasn't here to grumble at the boy and I just didn't care.

"Play what you want, honey," I said, sitting in Lionel's brown velvet recliner. Copies of *Downbeat* and packs of Trident were still stuffed between the cushion and the arm. Lion bounded off to his room and came back with an armful of tapes.

"Luther Vandross, Whitney Houston . . . what would you like to hear?"

"You pick." Even talking felt like too much work. He put on one of the tapes and I shut my eyes.

I hadn't expected to miss Lionel so much. We'd had twelve years together, eleven of them sober; we'd had Buster and raised the Lion, and we'd gone to the Grammys together when he was nominated and he'd stayed sober when he lost, and we'd made love, with more interest some years than others; we'd been through a few other women for him, a few blondes that he couldn't pass up, and one other man for me; I'm not criticizing. We knew each other so well that when I wrote a piece on another jazz musician, he'd find the one phrase and say, "You meant that about me," and he'd be right. He was a better father than your average musician; he brought us with him whenever he went to Europe, and no matter how late he played on Saturday, he got up and made breakfast on Sunday.

Maybe we weren't a perfect match, in age, or temperament, or color, but we did try and we were willing to stick it out and then we didn't get a chance.

Lion came and sat by me, putting his head against my knee. Just like Buster, I thought. Lion's mother was half Italian, like me, so the two boys look alike: creamier, silkier versions of their father.

I patted his hair and ran my thumb up and down his neck, feeling the muscles bunched up. When he was little, he couldn't fall asleep without his nightly back rub, and he only gave it up when he was fifteen and Lionel just wouldn't let me anymore.

"It's midnight, honey. It's been a long day, a long week. Go to bed."

He pushed his head against my leg and cried, the way men do, like it's being torn out of them. His tears ran down my bare leg, and I felt the strings holding me together just snap. One, two, three, and there was no more center.

"Go to bed, Lion."

"How about you?"

"I'm not really ready for bed yet, honey. Go ahead." Please, go to bed.

"Okay. Good night, Ma."

"Good night, baby." Nineteen-year-old baby.

He pulled himself up and went off to his room. I peered into the kitchen, looked at all the dishes, and closed my eyes again. After a while, I got up and finished off the little bit of Jim Beam left in the bottle. With all Lionel's efforts at sobriety, we didn't keep the stuff around, and I choked on it. But the burning in my throat was comforting, like old times, and it was a distraction.

I walked down the hall to the bedroom—I used to call it the Lionel Sampson Celebrity Shrine. It wasn't just his framed album covers, but all of his favorite reviews, including the ones I wrote before I met him; one of Billie's gardenias mounted on velvet, pressed behind glass; photos of Lionel playing with equally famous or more famous musicians or with famous fans. In some ways, it's easier to marry a man with a big ego; you're not always fretting over him, worrying about whether or not he needs fluffing up.

I threw my black dress on the floor, my worst habit, and got into bed. I woke up at around four, waiting for something. A minute later, Buster wandered in, eyes half shut, blue blankie resurrected and hung around his neck, like a little boxer.

"Gonna stay with you, Mama." Truculent even in his sleep, knowing that if his father had been there, he'd have been sent back to his own room.

"Come in, then, Bus. Let's try and get some sleep."

He curled up next to me, silently, an arm flung over me, the other arm thrust into his pajama bottoms, between his legs.

I had just shut my eyes again when I felt something out of place. Lion was standing in the doorway, his briefs hanging off his high skinny hips. He needed new underwear, I thought. He looked about a year older than Buster.

"I thought I heard Buster prowling around, y'know, sleepwalking."

The only one who ever sleepwalked in our family was Lion, but I didn't say so. "It's okay—he just wanted company. Lonely in this house tonight."

"Yeah. Ma?"

I was tired of thinking, and I didn't want to send him away, and I didn't want to talk anymore to anyone so I said, "Come on, honey, it's a big bed."

He crawled in next to his brother and fell asleep in a few minutes. I watched the digital clock flip through a lot of numbers and finally I got up and read.

The boys woke early, and I made them what Lionel called a Jersey City breakfast: eggs, sweet Italian sausage, grits, biscuits, and a quart of milk for each of them.

"Buster, soccer camp starts today. Do you feel up to going?"

I didn't see any reason for him to sit at home; he could catch up on his grieving for the rest of his life.

"I guess so. Is it okay, Mama?"

"Yes, honey, it's fine. I'm glad you're going. I'll pick you up at five, and then we'll drive straight over to Grandma's for dinner. You go get ready when you're done eating. Don't forget your cleats—they're in the hall."

Lion swallowed his milk and stood up, like a brown flamingo, balancing on one foot while he put on his sneaker. "Come on, Buster, I'm taking you. I have to go into town anyway. Do we need anything?"

I hadn't been to the grocery store in about a week. "Get milk and OJ and English muffins and American cheese. I'll do a real shop tomorrow." If I could just get to the store and the cleaners, then I could get to work, and then my life would move forward.

Finally they were ready to go, and I kissed them both and gave Lion some money for the groceries.

"I'll be back by lunchtime," he said. It was already eight-thirty. When his father got sick in the spring, Lion gave me hourly bulletins on his whereabouts. This summer, Lion was housepainting and home constantly, leaving late, back early, stopping by for lunch.

"If you like," I said. I didn't want him to feel that he had to keep me company. I was planning on going back to work tomorrow or the day after.

While the boys were gone, I straightened the house, went for a walk, and made curried tuna-fish sandwiches for Lion. I watched out the window for him, and when I saw my car turn up the road, I remembered all the things I hadn't done and started making a list. He came in, sweating and shirtless, drops of white paint on his hands and shoulders and sneakers.

Lion ate and I watched him and smiled. Feeding them was the easiest and clearest way of loving them, holding them.

"I'm going to shower. Then we could play a little tennis or work on the porch." He finished both sandwiches in about a minute and got that wistful look that teenage boys get when they want you to fix them something more to eat. I made two peanut-butter-and-jelly sandwiches and put them on his plate.

"Great. I don't have to work this afternoon," he said. "I told Joe I might not be back—he said okay."

"Well, I'm just going to mouse around, do laundry, answer some mail. I'm glad to have your company, you know I am, but you don't have to stay here with me. You might want to be with your friends."

"I don't. I'm gonna shower." Like his father, he only put his love out once, and God help you if you didn't take the hint.

I sat at the table, looking out at the morning glories climbing up the trellis Lionel had built me the summer he stopped drinking. In addition to the trellis, I had two flower boxes, a magazine rack, and a footstool so ugly even Ruth wouldn't have it.

"Ma, no towels," Lion shouted from the bathroom. I thought that was nice, as if real life might continue.

"All right," I called, getting one of the big, rough white ones that he liked.

I went into the bathroom and put it on the rack just as he stepped out of the shower. I hadn't seen him naked since he was fourteen and spent the year parading around the house, so that we could admire his underarm hair and the black wisps on his legs.

All I could see in the mist was a dark caramel column and two patches of dark curls, inky against his skin. I expected him to look away, embarrassed, but instead he looked right at me as he took the towel, and I was the one who turned away.

"Sorry," we both said, and I backed out of the bathroom and went straight down to the basement so we wouldn't bump into each other for a while.

I washed, dried, and folded everything that couldn't get away from me, listening for Lion's footsteps upstairs. I couldn't hear anything while the machines were going, so after about an hour I came up and found a note on the kitchen table.

Taking a nap. Wake me when it's time to get Buster. L.

"L.," is how his father used to sign his notes. And their handwriting was the same, too: the awkward, careful printing of men who know that their script is illegible.

I took a shower and dried my hair and looked in the mirror for a while, noticing the gray at the temples. I wondered what Lion would have seen if he'd walked in on me, and I made up my mind not to think like that again.

I woke Lion by calling him from the hall, and I went into my room while he dressed to go to his grandmother's. I found a skirt that was somber and ill-fitting enough to meet Ruth's standard of widowhood and thought about topping it off with my EIGHT TO THE BAR VOLLEYBALL CHAMPS T-shirt, but didn't. Even pulling Ruth's chain wasn't fun. I put on a yellow shirt that made me look like one of the Neapolitan cholera victims, and Lion and I went to get Buster. He was bubbling over about the goal he had made in the last quarter, and that filled the car until we got to Ruth's house, and then she took over.

"Come in, come in. Gabriel, you are too dirty to be my grandson. You go wash up right now. Lionel junior, you're looking a little peaked. You must be working too hard or playing too hard. Does he eat, Julia? Come sit down here and have a glass of nice iced tea with mint from my garden. Julia, guess who I heard from this afternoon? Loretta, Lionel's first wife. She called to say how sorry she was. I told her she could call upon you, if she wished."

"Fine." I didn't have the energy to be annoyed. My muscles felt like butter, I'd had a headache for six days, and my eyes were so sore that even when I closed them, they ached. If Ruth wanted to sic Loretta McVay Sampson de Guzman de God-knows-who-else on me, I guessed I'd get through that little hell, too.

Ruth looked at me, probably disappointed; I knew from Lionel that she couldn't stand Loretta, but since she was the *only* black woman he'd married, Ruth felt obliged to find something positive about her. She was a lousy singer, a whore, and a terrible housekeeper, so Ruth really had to search. Anita, wife number two, was a rich, pretty flake with a fragile air and a serious drug problem that killed her when the Lion was five. I was the only normal, functioning person Lionel was ever involved with: I worked, I cooked, I balanced our checkbook, I did what had to be done, just like Ruth. And I irritated her no end.

"Why'd you do that, Grandma? Loretta's so nasty. She probably just wants to find out if Pop left her something in his will, which I'm sure he did not." Loretta and Lionel had had a little thing going when Anita was in one of her rehab centers, and I think the Lion found out and of course blamed Loretta.

"It's all right, Lion," I said, and stopped myself from patting his hand as if he were Buster.

Ruth was offended. "Really, young man, it was very decent, just common courtesy, for Loretta to pay her respects, and I'm sure that your stepmother appreciates that." Ruth thought it disrespectful to call me Julia when talking to Lion, but she couldn't stand the fact that he called me Ma after the four years she put in raising him while Anita killed herself and Lionel toured. So she referred to me as "your stepmother," which always made me feel like the coachmen and pumpkins couldn't be far behind. Lion used to look at me and smile when she said it.

We got through dinner, with Buster bragging about soccer and giving us a minute-by-minute account of the soccer training movie he had seen. Ruth criticized their table manners, asked me how long I was going to wallow at home, and then expressed horror when I told her I was going to work on Monday. Generally, she was her usual self, just a little worse, which was true of the rest of us, too. She also served the best smothered pork chops ever made and her usual first-rate trimmings. She brightened up when the boys both asked for seconds and I praised her pork chops and the sweet-potato soufflé for a solid minute.

After dinner, I cleared and the two of us washed and dried while the boys watched TV. I never knew how to talk to Ruth; my father-in-law was the easy one, and when Alfred died I lost my biggest fan. I looked over at Ruth, scrubbing neatly stacked pots with her pink rubber gloves, which matched her pink-and-white apron, which had nothing cute or whimsical about it. She hadn't raised Lionel to be a good husband; she'd raised him to be a warrior, a god, a genius surrounded by courtiers. But I married him anyway, when he was too old to be a warrior, too tired to be a god, and smart enough to know the limits of his talent.

I thought about life without my boys, and I gave Ruth a little hug as she was tugging off her gloves. She humphed and wiped her hands on her apron.

"You take care of yourself, now. Those boys need you more than ever." She walked into the living room and announced that it was time for us to go, since she had a church meeting.

We all thanked her, and I drove home with three pink Tupperware containers beside me. The car smelled like pork chop.

I wanted to put Buster to bed, but it was only eight o'clock. I let him watch some sitcoms and changed out of my clothes and into my bathrobe. Lion came into the hall in a fresh shirt.

"Going out?" He looked so pretty in his clean white shirt.

"Yeah, some of the guys want to go down to the Navigator. I said I'd stop by, see who's there. Don't wait up."

I was surprised but delighted. I tossed him the keys. "Okay, drive carefully."

Buster got himself into pajamas and even brushed his teeth without my nagging him. He had obviously figured out that I was not operating at full speed. I tucked him in, trying to give him enough hugs and kisses to help him get settled, not so many that he'd hang on my neck for an extra fifteen minutes. I went to sit in the kitchen, staring at the moths smacking themselves against the screen door. I could relate to that.

I read a few magazines, plucked my eyebrows, thought about plucking the gray hairs at my temples, and decided not to bother. Who'd look? Who'd mind, except me?

Finally, I got into bed, and got out about twenty minutes later. I poured myself some bourbon and tried to go to sleep again, thinking that I hadn't ever really appreciated what it took Lionel to get through life sober. I woke up at around four, anticipating Buster. But there, leaning against the doorway, was Lion.

"Ma." He sounded congested.

"Are you all right?"

"Yeah. No. Can I come in?"

"Of course, come in. What is it, honey?"

He sat on the bed and plucked at my blanket, and I could smell the beer and the sweat coming off him. I sat up so we could talk, and he threw his arms around me like a drowning man. He was crying and gasping into my neck, and then he stopped and just rested his head against my shoulder. I kept on patting his back, rubbing the long muscles under the satiny skin. My hands were cold against his warm skin.

Lion lifted his head and looked into my eyes, his own eyes like pools of coffee, shining in the moonlight. He put his hand up to my cheek, and then he kissed me and my brain stopped. I shut my eyes.

His kisses were sweet and slow; he pushed his tongue into my mouth just a little at a time, getting more confident every time. He began to rub my nipples through my nightgown, spreading the fingers on one big hand wide apart just as his father used to, and I pulled away, forcing my eyes open.

"No, Lion. You have to go back to your room now." But I was asking him, I wasn't telling him, and I knew he wouldn't move.

"No." And he put his soft plummy mouth on my breast, soaking the nightgown. "Please don't send me away." The right words.

I couldn't send my little boy away, so I wrapped my arms around him and pulled him to me, out of the darkness.

It had been a long time since I was in bed with a young man. Lionel was forty-two when I met him, and before that I'd been living with a sax player eight years older than I was. I hadn't made love to anyone this young since I was seventeen and too young myself to appreciate it.

His body was so smooth and supple, and the flesh clung to the bone; when he was above me, he looked like an athlete working out; below me, he looked like an angel spread out for the world's adoration. His shoulders had clefts so deep I could lay a finger in each one, and each of his ribs stuck out just a little. He hadn't been eating enough at school. I couldn't move forward or backward, and so I shut my eyes again, so as not to see and not to have to think the same sad, tired thoughts.

He rose and fell between my hips and it reminded me of Buster's birth: heaving and sliding and then an explosive push. Lion apologized the way men do when they come too soon, and I hugged him and felt almost like myself, comforting him. I couldn't speak at all; I didn't know if I'd ever have a voice again.

He was whispering, "I love you, I love you, I love you." And I put my hand over his mouth until he became quiet. He tried to cradle me, pulling my head to his shoulder. I couldn't lie with him like that, so I wriggled away in the dark, my arms around my pillow. I heard him sigh, and then he laid his head on my back. He fell asleep in a minute.

I got up before either of them, made a few nice-neighbor phone calls, and got Buster a morning playdate, lunch included, and a ride to soccer camp. He was up, dressed, fed, and over to the Bergs' before Lion opened his eyes.

Lion's boss called and said he was so sorry for our loss but could Lionel junior please come to work this morning.

I put my hand on Lion's shoulder to wake him, and I could see the shock and the pleasure in his eyes. I told him he was late for work and laid his clothes out on his bed. He kept opening his mouth to say something, but I gave him toast and coffee and threw him my keys.

"You're late, Lion. We'll talk when you get home."

"I'm not sorry," he said, and I could have smiled. Good, I thought, spend the day not being sorry, because sometime after that you're gonna feel like shit. I was already sorrier than I'd ever been in my whole life, sorry enough for this life and the next. Lion looked at me and then at the keys in his hand.

"I guess I'll go. Ma . . . Julia . . ."

I was suddenly, ridiculously angry at being called Julia. "Go, Lion."

He was out the door. I started breathing again, trying to figure out how to save us both. Obviously, I couldn't be trusted to take care of him; I'd have to send him away. I thought about sending Buster away, too, but I didn't think I could. And maybe my insanity was limited to the Lion, maybe I could still act like a normal mother to Buster.

I called my friend Jeffrey in Falmouth and told him Lion needed a change of scene. He said Lion could start housepainting tomorrow and could stay with him since his kids were away. The whole time I was talking, I cradled the bottle of bourbon in my left arm, knowing that if I couldn't get through the phone call, or the afternoon, or the rest of my life, I had some help. I think I was so good at helping Lionel quit drinking because I didn't have the faintest idea why he, or anybody, drank. If I met him now, I'd be a better wife but not better for him. I packed Lion's suitcase and put it under his bed.

When I was a lifeguard at camp, they taught us how to save panicky swimmers. The swimmers don't realize that they have to let you save them, that their terror will drown you both, and so sometimes, they taught us, you have to knock the person out to bring him in to shore.

I practiced my speech in the mirror and on the porch and while making the beds. I thought if I said it clearly and quietly he would understand, and I could deliver him to Jeffrey, ready to start his summer over again. I went to the grocery store and bought weird, disconnected items: marinated artichoke hearts for Lionel, who was dead; red caviar to make into dip for his son, whose life I had just ruined; peanut butter with the grape jelly already striped into it for Buster, as a special treat that he would probably have outgrown by the time I got home; a pack of Kools for me, who stopped smoking fifteen years ago. I also bought a wood-refinishing kit, a jar of car wax, a six-pack of Michelob Light, five TV dinners, some hamburger but no buns, and a box of Pop-Tarts. Clearly the cart of a woman at the end of her rope.

Lion came home at three, and I could see him trying to figure out how to tackle me. He sat down at the kitchen table and frowned when I didn't say anything.

I sat down across from him, poured us each a glass of bourbon, and lit a cigarette, which startled him. All the props said "Important Moment."

"Let me say what I have to say and then you can tell me whatever you want to. Lion, I love you very much and I have felt blessed to be your mother and I've probably ruined that for both of us. Just sit still. What happened was not your fault; you were upset, you didn't know. . . . Nothing would have happened if I had been my regular self. But anyway . . ."This was going so badly I just wanted to finish my cigarette and take the boy to the train station, whether he understood or not. "I think you'd feel a lot better and clearer if you had some time away, so I talked to Jeffrey—"

"No. No, goddammit, I am not leaving and I wasn't upset—it was what I wanted. You can't send me away. I'm not a kid anymore. You can leave me, but you can't make me leave." He was charging around the kitchen, bumping into the chairs, blind.

I just sat there. All of a sudden, he was finding his voice, the one I had always tried to nurture, to find a place for between his father's roar and his brother's contented hum. I was hearing his debut as a man, and now I had to keep him down and raise him up at the same time.

"How can it be so easy for you to send me away? Don't you love me at all?"

I jumped up, glad to have a reason to move. "Not love you? It's because I love you, because I want you to have a happy, normal life. I owe it to you and I owe it to your father."

He folded his arms. "You don't owe Pop anything. . . . He had everything he wanted, he had everything."The words rained down like little blades.

I ignored what he said. "It can't be, honey. You can't stay."

"I could if you wanted me to."

He was right. Who would know? I could take my two boys to the movies, away for weekends, play tennis with my stepson. I would be the object of a little pity and some admiration. Who would know? Who would have such monstrous thoughts, except Ruth, and she would never allow them to surface. I saw us together and saw it unfolding, leaves of shame and pity and anger, neither of us getting what we wanted. I wanted to hug him, console him for his loss.

"No, honey."

I reached across the table but he shrugged me off, grabbing my keys and heading out the door.

I sat for a long time, sipping, watching the sunlight move around the kitchen. When it was almost five, I took the keys from Lionel's side of the dresser and drove his van to soccer camp. Buster felt like being quiet, so we just held hands and listened to the radio. I offered to take him to Burger King, hoping the automated monkeys and video games would be a good substitute for a fully present and competent mother. He was happy, and we killed an hour and a half there. Three hours to bedtime.

We watched some TV, sitting on the couch, his feet in my lap. Every few minutes, I'd look at the clock on the mantel and then promise myself I wouldn't look until the next commercial. Every time I started to move, I'd get tears in my eyes, so I concentrated on sitting very still, waiting for time to pass. Finally, I got Buster through his nightly routine and into bed, kissing his cupcake face, fluffing his Dr. J pillow.

"Where's Lion? He said he'd kiss me good night."

"Honey, he's out. He'll come in and kiss you while you're sleeping. "

"Where is he?"

I dug my nails into my palms; with Buster, this could go on for half an hour. "He's out with some friends, Bus. I promise he'll kiss you in your sleep."

"Okay. I'm glad he's home, Mama."

How had I managed to do so much harm so fast? "I know. Go to sleep, Gabriel Tyner Sampson."

"G'night, Mama. Say my full name again."

"Gabriel Tyner Sampson, beautiful name for a beautiful boy. 'Night."

And I thought about the morning we named him, holding him in the delivery room, his boneless brown body covered with white goop and clots of blood, and Lionel tearing off his green mask to kiss me and then to kiss the baby, rubbing his face all over Gabriel's little body.

I got into my kimono and sat in the rocking chair, waiting for Lion. I watched the guests on the talk shows, none of whom seemed like people I'd want to know. After a while, I turned off the sound but kept the picture on for company. I watered my plants, then realized I had just done it yesterday and watched as the water cascaded out of the pots onto the wood floor, drops bouncing onto the wall, streaking the white paint. I thought about giving away the plants, or maybe moving somewhere where people didn't keep plants. Around here, it's like a law. The mopping up took me about eight minutes, and I tried to think of something else to do. I looked for a dish to break.

Stupid, inconsiderate boy. Around now, his father would have been pacing, threatening to beat him senseless when he walked in, and I would have been calming Lionel down, trying to get him to come to bed.

At about three, when I was thinking of calling the hospital, I heard my car coming up the street slowly. I looked out the kitchen window and saw him pull into the drive, minus the right front fender.

He came inside quietly, pale gray around his mouth and eyes. There was blood on his shirt, but he was walking okay. I grabbed him by the shoulders and he winced and I dug my hands into him in the dark of the hallway.

"What is wrong with you? I don't have enough to contend with? Do you know it's three o'clock in the morning? There were no phones where you were, or what? It was too inconvenient to call home, to tell me you weren't lying dead somewhere? Am I talking to myself, goddammit?"

I was shaking him hard, wanting him to talk back so I could slap his face, and he was crying, turning his face away from me. I pulled him into the light of the kitchen and saw the purple bruise, the shiny puff of skin above his right eyebrow. There was a cut in his upper lip, making it lift and twist like a harelip.

"What the hell happened to you?"

"I got into a little fight at the Navigator and then I had sort of an accident, nothing serious. I just hit a little tree and bumped my head."

"You are an asshole."

"I know, Ma, I'm sorry. I'll pay you back for the car so your insurance won't go up. I'm really sorry."

I put my hands in my pockets and waited for my adrenaline to subside.

I steered him into the bathroom and sat him down on the toilet while I got some ice cubes and wrapped them in a dish towel; that year I was always making compresses for Buster's skinned knees, busted lips, black eyes. Lion sat there holding the ice to his forehead. The lip was too far gone.

I wasn't angry anymore and I said so. He smiled lopsidedly and leaned against me for a second. I moved away and told him to wash up.

"All right, I'll be out in a minute."

"Take your time."

I sat on the couch, thinking about his going away and whether or not Jeffrey would be good company for him. Lion came out of the bathroom without his bloody shirt, the dish towel in his hand. He stood in the middle of the room, like he didn't know where to sit, and then he eased down onto the couch, tossing the towel from hand to hand.

"Don't send me away. I don't want to go away from you and Grandma and Buster. I just can't leave home this summer. Please, Ma, it won't—what happened won't happen again. Please let me stay home." He kept looking at his hands, smoothing the towel over his knees and then balling it up.

How could I do that to him?

"All right, let's not talk about it any more tonight."

He put his head back on the couch and sighed, sliding over so his cheek was on my shoulder. I patted his good cheek and went to sit in the brown chair.

I started to say more, to explain to him how it was going to be, but then I thought I shouldn't. I would tell him that we were looking at wreckage and he would not want to know.

I said good night and went to my bedroom. He was still on the couch in the morning.

We tried for a few weeks, but toward the end of the summer Lion got so obnoxious I could barely speak to him. Ruth kept an uncertain peace for the first two weeks and then blew up at him. "Where have your manners gone, young man? After all she did for you, this is the thanks she gets? And Julia, when did you get so mush-mouthed that you can't tell him to behave himself?" Lion and I looked at our plates, and Ruth stared at us, puzzled and cross. I came home from work on a Friday and found a note on the kitchen table: *Friends called with a housepainting job in Nantucket. Will call before I go to Paris. Will still do junior year abroad, if that's okay. L.* "If that's okay" meant that he wanted me to foot the bill, and I did. I would have done more if I had known how.

It's almost summer again. Buster and I do pretty well, and we have dinner every Sunday with Ruth, and more often than not, we drive her over to bingo on Thursday evenings and play a few games ourselves. I see my husband everywhere; in the deft hands of the man handing out the bingo cards, in the black-olive eyes of the boy sitting next to me on the bench, in the thick, curved back of the man moving my new piano. I am starting to play again and I'm teaching Buster.

Most nights, after I have gone to bed, I find myself in the living room or standing on the porch in the cold night air. I tell myself that I am not waiting, it's just that I'm not yet awake.

NIGHT VISION

For fifteen years, I saw my stepmother only in my dreams.

After my father got sick in the spring of my sophomore year, dying fast and ugly in the middle of June, I went to Paris to recover, to become someone else, *un homme du monde,* an expert in international maritime law, nothing like the college boy who slept with his stepmother the day after his father's funeral. We grieved apart after that night, and I left Julia to raise my little brother, Buster, and pay all the bills, including mine. Buster shuttled back and forth for holidays, even as a grown man, calm and affectionate with us both, bringing me Deaf Smith County peanut butter from my mother for Christmas morning, carrying home jars of Fauchon jam from me, packed in three of his sweat socks. My mother's letters came on the first of every month for fifteen years, news of home, of my soccer coach's retirement, newspaper clippings about maritime law and French shipping lines, her new address in Massachusetts, a collection of her essays on jazz. I turned the book over and learned that her hair had turned gray.

"You gotta come home, Lionel," my brother said last time, his wife sprawled beside him on my couch, her long, pretty feet resting on his crotch.

"I don't think so."

"She misses you. You know that. You should go see her."

Jewelle nodded, digging her feet a little further, and Buster grinned hugely and closed his eyes.

"You guys," I said.

My brother married someone more beautiful and wild than I would have chosen. They had terrible, flying-dishes fights and passionate reconciliations every few months, and they managed to divorce and remarry in one year, without even embarrassing themselves. Jewelle loved Buster to death and told me she only left when he needed leaving, and my brother would say in her defense that it was nothing less than the truth. He never said what he had done that would deserve leaving, and I can't think that it was anything very bad. There is no bad even in the depths of Buster's soul, and when I am sick of him, his undaunted, fat-and-sassy younger-brotherness, I think that there are no depths.

When Buster and Jewelle were together (usually Columbus Day through July Fourth weekend), happiness poured out of them. Buster showed slides of Jewelle's artwork, thickly layered slashes of dark paint, and Jewelle cooked platters of fried chicken and bragged on his triumphs as a public defender. When they were apart, they both lost weight and shine and acted like people in the final stage of terminal heartbreak. Since Jewelle's arrival in Buster's life, I have had a whole secondhand love affair and passionate marriage, and in return Buster got use of my apartment in New York and six consecutive Labor Days in Paris.

"Ma misses you," he said again. He held Jewelle's feet in one hand. "You know she does. She's getting old."

"I definitely don't believe that. She's fifty, fifty-five. That's not old. We'll be there ourselves in no time."

My mother, my stepmother, my only mother, is fifty-four and I am thirty-four and it has comforted me over the years to picture myself in what I expect to be a pretty vigorous middle age and to contemplate poor Julia tottering along, nylon knee-highs sloshing around her ankles, chin hairs and dewlaps flapping in the breeze.

"Fine. She's a spring chicken." Buster cut four inches of Brie and chewed on it. "She's not a real young fifty-five. What did she do so wrong, Lionel? Tell me. I know she loves you, I know she loves me. She loved Pop; she saved his life as far as I can tell. Jesus, she took care of Grammy Ruth for three years when anyone else would've put a pillow over the woman's face. Ma is really a good person, and whatever has pissed you off, you could let it go now. You know, she can't help being white."

Jewelle, of whom we could say the same thing, pulled her feet out of his hand and curled her toes over his waistband, under his round belly.

"If she died tomorrow, how sorry would you be?" she said.

Buster and I stared at her, brothers again, because in our family you did not say things like that, not even with good intentions.

I poured wine for us all and passed around the fat green olives Jewelle liked.

"Well. Color is not the issue. You can tell her I'll come in June."

Buster went into my bedroom. "I'm calling Ma," he said. "I'm telling her June."

Jewelle gently spat olive pits into her hand and shaped them into a neat pyramid on the coffee table.

I flew home with my new girlfriend, Claudine, and her little girl, Mirabelle. Claudine had business and a father in Boston, and a small hotel and me in Paris. She was lean as a boy and treated me with wry Parisian affection, as if all kisses were mildly amusing if one gave it any thought. Claudine's consistent, insouciant aridity was easy on me; I'd come to prefer my lack of intimacy straight up. Mirabelle was my true sweetheart. I loved her orange cartoon curls, her red glasses, and her welterweight swagger. She was Ma Poupée and I was her Bel Homme.

Claudine's father left a new black Crown Victoria for us at Logan, with chocolates and a Tintin comic on the backseat and Joan Sutherland in the CD player. Claudine folded up her black travel sweater and hung a white linen jacket on the back hook. There was five hundred dollars in the glove compartment, and I was apparently the only one who thought that if you were lucky enough to have a father, you might reasonably expect him to meet you at the airport after a two-year separation. My father would have been at that gate, drunk or sober. Mirabelle kicked the back of the driver's seat all the way from the airport, singing what the little boy from Dallas had taught her on the flight over: "*I'm* gonna kick you. I'm *gonna* kick you. I'm gonna *kick* you. I'm gonna kick *you,* right in your big old heinie." Claudine watched out the window until I pulled onto the turnpike, and then she closed her eyes. Anything in English was my department.

I recognized the new house right away. My mother had dreamed and sketched its front porch and its swing a hundred times during my childhood, on every telephone-book cover and notepad we ever had. For years my father talked big about a glass-and-steel house on the water, recording studio overlooking the ocean, wraparound deck for major partying and jam sessions, and for years I sat next to him on the couch while he read the paper and I read the funnies and we listened to my mother tuck my brother in: "Once upon a time, there were two handsome princes, Prince Fric, who was a little older, and Prince Frac, who was a little younger. They lived with their parents, the King and Queen, in a beautiful little cottage with a beautiful front porch looking out over the River Wilde. They lived in the little cottage because a big old castle with a wraparound deck and a million windows is simply more trouble than it's worth."

Julia stood before us on the porch, both arms upraised, her body pale and square in front of an old willow, its branches pooling on the lawn. Claudine pulled off her sunglasses and said, "You don't resemble her," and I explained, as I thought I had several times between rue de Birague and the Massachusetts border, that this was my stepmother, that my real mother had died when I was five and Julia had married my father and adopted me. "Ah," said Claudine, "not your real mother."

Mirabelle said, *"Qu'est-ce que c'est, ca?"*

"Tire swing," I said.

Claudine said, "May I smoke?"

"I don't know. She used to smoke."

"Did she stop?"

"I don't know. I don't know if she smokes or not, Claudine."

She reached for her jacket. "Does your mother know I'm coming?"

"Here we are, Poupée," I said to Mirabelle.

I stood by the car and watched my mother make a fuss over Mirabelle's red hair (speaking pretty good French, which I had never heard) and turn Claudine around to admire the crispness of her jacket. She shepherded us up the steps, thanking us for the gigantic and unimaginative bottle of toilet water. Claudine went into the bathroom; Mirabelle went out to the swing. My mother and I stood in her big white kitchen. She hadn't touched me.

"Bourbon?" she said.

"It's midnight in Paris, too late for me."

"Right," my mother said. "Gin and tonic?"

We were just clinking our glasses when Claudine came out and asked for water and an ashtray.

"No smoking in the house, Claudine. I'm sorry."

Claudine shrugged in that contemptuous way Parisians do, so wildly disdainful you have to laugh or hit them. She went outside, lighting up before she was through the door. We touched glasses again.

"Maybe you didn't know I was bringing a friend?" I said.

My mother smiled. "Buster didn't mention it."

"Do you mind?"

"I don't mind. You might have been bringing her to meet me. I don't think you did, but you might have. And a very cute kid. Really adorable."

"And Claudine?"

"Very pretty. *Chien*. That's the word I remember, I don't know if they still say that."

Chien means a bitchy, stylish appeal. They do still say that, and my own landlady has said it of Claudine.

Julia dug her hands into a bowl of tarragon and cream cheese and pushed it, one little white gob at a time, under the skin of the big chicken sitting on the counter. "Do you cook?"

"I do. I'm a good cook. Like Pop."

My mother put the chicken in the oven and laughed. "Honey, what did your father ever cook?"

"He was a good cook. He made those big breakfasts on Sunday, he barbecued great short ribs—I remember those."

"Oh, Abyssinian ribs. I remember them, too. Those were some great parties in those bad old days. Even after he stopped drinking, your father was really fun at a party." She smiled as if he were still in the room.

My father was a madly friendly, kissy, unreliable drunk when I was a little boy, and a successful, dependable musician and father after he met Julia. Once she became my mother, I never worried about him, I never hid again from that red-eyed, wet-lipped stranger, but I did occasionally miss the old drunk.

Claudine stuck her head back into the kitchen, beautiful and squinting through her smoke, and Mirabelle ran in beneath her. My mother handed her two carrots and a large peeler with a black spongy handle for arthritic cooks, and Mirabelle flourished it at us both, our little musketeer. My mother brought out three less fancy peelers, and while we worked our way through a good-size pile of carrots and pink potatoes, she told us how she met my father at Barbara Cook's house and how they both ditched their dates, my mother leaving behind her favorite coat. Claudine told us about the lady who snuck twin Siamese bluepoints into the hotel in her ventilated Vuitton trunk and bailed out on her bill, taking six towels and leaving the cats behind. Claudine laughed at my mother's story and shook her head over the lost red beaver jacket, and my mother laughed at Claudine's story and shook her head over people's foolishness. Mirabelle fished the lime out of Claudine's club soda and sucked on it.

A feeling of goodwill and confidence settled on me for no reason I can imagine.

"Hey," I said, "let's stay over. Here."

My mother smiled and looked at Claudine.

"Perhaps we will just see how we feel," Claudine said. "I am a little *fatiguée.*"

"Why don't you take a nap before dinner," my mother and I said simultaneously.

"Perhaps," she said, and kept peeling.

I think now that I must have given Claudine the wrong impression, that she'd come expecting a doddering old lady, none too sharp or tidy these days, living on dented canned goods and requiring a short, sadly empty visit before she collapsed entirely. Julia, with a silver braid hanging down her broad back, in black T-shirt, black pants, and black two-dollar flip-flops on her wide coral-tipped feet, was not that old lady at all.

My mother gave Mirabelle a bowl of cut-up vegetables to put on the table, and she carried it like treasure, the pink radishes bobbing among the ice cubes. Claudine waved her hand around, wanting another cigarette, and my mother gave her a glass of red wine. Claudine put it down a good ten inches away from her.

"I am sorry. We have reservations. Lionel, will you arrange your car? Mirabelle and me must go after dinner. Thank you, Madame Sampson, for your kindness."

My mother lifted her glass to Claudine. "Anytime. I hope you both come again." She did not say anything like "Oh no, my dear, please stay here," or "Lionel, you can't let Claudine drive into Boston all by herself." I poured myself another drink. I'm still surprised I didn't offer to drive, because I was brought up properly, and because I had been sure until the moment Mirabelle pulled the lime out of Claudine's glass that I wanted to stay at the Ritz in Boston, that I had come only so that I could depart.

Mirabelle told my mother the long story of the airplane meal and the spilled soda and the nice lady and the bad little boy from Texas and Monsieur Teddy's difficult flight squashed in a suitcase with a hiking boot pressed against his nose for seven hours. My mother laughed and admired and clucked sympathetically in all the right places, passing the platter of chicken and bowls of cucumber salad and minted peas. She poured another grenadine and ginger ale for Mirabelle, who watched the bubbles rise through the fuchsia syrup. She had just reached for her glass when Claudine arranged her knife and fork on her plate and stood up.

Mirabelle sighed, tilting her head back to drain her drink, like one of my father's old buddies at closing time. We all watched her swallow. My mother made very strong coffee for Claudine, filling an old silver thermos and putting together a plastic-wrapped mound of lemon squares for the road. She doted on Mirabelle and deferred to Claudine as if they were my lovable child and my formidable wife and she my fond and familiar mother. She refused to let us clear the table and amused Mirabelle while Claudine changed into comfortable driving clothes.

Mirabelle and my mother kissed good-bye French-style, and then Claudine did the same, walking out the kitchen door without waiting to see if I followed, which, of course, I did. I didn't want to be, I wasn't, rude or uninterested; I just didn't want to leave yet. Mirabelle hugged me quickly and lay down on the backseat. I made a little sweater pillow for her, and she brushed her cheek against my hand. Claudine made a big production of adjusting the Crown Victoria's side mirror, the rearview mirror, and the seat belt.

"Do you know how to get to the city?" I asked in French.

"Yes."

"And then you stay on—"

"I have a map," she said. "I can sleep by the side of the road until morning if I get lost."

"That probably won't be necessary. You have five hundred dollars in cash and seven credit cards. There'll be a hundred motels in the next fifty miles."

"We'll be fine. I will take care of everything," she said. In very fast English she added, "Do not call me, all right? We can speak to each other when you get back to Paris, perhaps."

"Okay, Claudine. Take it easy. I'm sorry. I'll call you in a few weeks. Mirabelle, *dors bien, fais de beaux rêves, mon ange.*"

I watched them drive off, and I watched the fat white moon hanging over my mother's roof. I was scared to go back into the house. I called out, "Where's Buster? I thought he was coming up." I had threatened not to come back if my brother didn't show up within twenty-four hours.

My mother stuck her head out the front door. "He'll be here tomorrow. He's jammed up in court. He said dinner at the latest."

"With or without the Jewelle?"

"With. Very much with. It's only June, you know."

"You don't think she gives Bus a little too much action?"

"I don't think he's looking for peace. He's peaceful enough. I think he was looking for a wild ride and she gives it to him. And she does love him to death."

"I know. She's kind of a nut, Ma."

And it didn't matter what we said then, because my lips calling her mother, her heart hearing mother after so long, blew across the bright night sky and stirred the long branches of the willow tree.

"Are you coming in?" she said.

"In a few."

"In a few I'll be asleep. You can finish cleaning up."

I heard her overhead, her heavy step on the stairs, the creak of her bedroom floor, the double thump of the bathroom door, which I had noticed needed fixing. I thought about changing the hinges on that door, and I thought of my mouth around her hard nipple, her wet nightgown over my tongue, a tiny bubble of cotton I had to rip the nightgown to get rid of. She had reached over me to click off the light, and the last thing I saw that night was the white underside of her arm. In the dark she smelled of honey and salt and the faint tang of wet metal.

I washed the wineglasses by hand and wiped down the counters. When my father was rehearsing and my brother was noodling around in his room, when I wasn't too busy with soccer and school, my mother and I cleaned up the kitchen and listened to music. We talked or we didn't, and she did some old Moms Mabley routines and I did Richard Pryor, and we stayed in the kitchen until about ten.

I called upstairs.

"Do you mind living alone?"

My mother stood at the top of the stairs in a man's blue terry-cloth robe and blue fuzzy slippers the size of small dogs.

"Sweet Jesus, it *is* Moms Mabley," I said.

"No hat," she said.

I realized, a little late, that it was not a kind thing to say to a middle-aged woman.

"And I've still got my teeth. I put towels in the room at the end of the hall. The bed's made up. I'll be up before you in the morning."

"How do you know?"

"I don't know." She came down three steps. "I'm pretending I know. But it is true that I get up earlier than most people. I can make you an omelet if you want."

"I'm not much of a breakfast man."

She smiled, and then her smile folded up and she put her hand over her mouth.

"Ma, it's all right."

"I hope so, honey. Not that—I'm still sorry." She sat down on the stairs, her robe pulled tight under her thighs.

"It's all right." I poured us both a little red wine and handed it to her, without going up the stairs. "So, do you mind living alone?"

My mother sighed. "Not so much. I'm a pain in the ass. I could live with a couple of other old ladies, I guess. Communal potlucks and watching who's watering down the gin. It doesn't really sound so bad. Maybe in twenty years."

"Maybe you'll meet someone."

"Maybe. I think I'm pretty much done meeting people."

"You're only fifty-five. You're the same age as Tina Turner."

"Yup. And Tina is probably tired of meeting people, too. How about you—do you mind living alone?"

"I don't exactly live alone—"

"You do. That's exactly what you do—you live alone. And have relationships with people who are very happy to let you live alone."

"Claudine's really a lot of fun, Ma. You didn't get to know her."

"She may be a whole house of fun, but don't tell me she inspires thoughts of a happy domestic life."

"No."

"That little girl could."

I told her a few of my favorite Mirabelle stories, and she told me stories I had forgotten about me and my brother drag-racing shopping carts down Cross Street, locking our babysitter in the basement, stretching ourselves on the doorways, and praying to be tall.

"We never made you guys say your prayers, we certainly never went to church, and we kept you far away from Grammy Ruth's Never Forgive Never Forget Pentecostal Church of the Holy Fruitcakes. And there you two would be, on your knees to Jesus, praying to be six feet tall."

"It worked," I said.

"It did." She stretched her legs down a few steps, and I saw that they were unchanged, still smooth and tan, with hard calves that squared when she moved.

"You ought to think about marrying again," I said.

"You ought to think about doing it the first time."

"Well, let's get on it. Let's find people to marry. Broomstick-jumping time in Massachusetts and Paree."

My mother stood up. "You do it, honey. You find someone smart and funny and kindhearted and get married so I can make a fuss over the grandbabies."

I saluted her with the wineglass. "Yes, ma'am."

"Good night. Sleep tight."

"Good night, Ma."

I waited until I heard the toilet flush and the faucets shut, and I listened to her walk across her bedroom and heard her robe drop on the floor, and I could even hear her quilt settle down upon her. I drank in a serious way, which I rarely do, until I thought I could sleep. I made to lay my glasses on the rickety nightstand and dropped them on the floor near my clothes. Close enough, I thought, and lay down and had to sit up immediately, my eyes seeming to float out of my head, my stomach rising and falling in great waves of gin and Merlot. Stubbing my toe on the bathroom doorframe, I reached for the light switch and knocked over a water glass. I knew that broken glass lay all around me, although I couldn't see it, and I toe-danced backward toward the bed, twirling and leaping to safety. I reached for my glasses, hiding on the blue rug near my jeans, and somehow rammed my balls into the pink and brown Billie Holiday lamp. I fell to the floor, hoping for no further damage and complete unconsciousness.

My naked mother ran into the room. I was curled up in a ball, her feet beside my ass. She knelt down, pushing back my hair to get a better look at me. Her breasts swung down, half in, half out of the hallway's dusty light.

"You do not have a scratch on you," she said, and patted my cheek. "Walk over toward the door—there's nothing that way. I'll get a broom."

I could see her, both more and less clearly than I would have liked. She pushed herself up, and the view of her folded belly and still-dark pubic hair was replaced by the sharp swing of her hips, wider now, tenderly pulled down at the soft bottom edges, but still that same purposeful, kick-down-the-door walk.

She came back in her robe and slippers, with a broom and dustpan, and I wrapped a towel around my waist. I stood up straight so that even if she needed glasses as much as I did what she saw of me would look good.

"Quite the event. Is there something, some small thing in this room, you didn't run into?"

"No," I said. "I think I've made contact with almost everything. The armchair stayed out of my way, but otherwise, for a low-key kind of guy, I'd have to say I got the job done."

My mother dumped the pieces of glass and the lightbulb and the lamp remains into the wastebasket.

"You smell like the whole Napa Valley," she said, "so I won't offer you a brandy."

"I don't usually drink this way, Ma. I'm sorry for the mess."

She put down the broom and the dustpan and came over to me and smiled at my towel. She put her lips to the middle of my chest, over my beating heart.

"I love you past speech."

We stood there, my long neck bent down to her shoulder, her hands kneading my back. We breathed in and out together.

"I'll say good night, honey. Quite a day."

She waved one hand over her shoulder and walked away.

LIGHT INTO DARK

"It's six-fifteen," Lionel says to his stepmother. "Decent people have started drinking."

"Maybe I should put out some food," Julia says.

Lionel nods, looking around for the little cluster of liquor bottles Julia had thrown out when his father was alive and trying to stay sober, and which she replaced on the sideboard as soon as the man passed away. Lionel's not sorry he's dragged himself and his stepson from Paris to Massachusetts for their first trip together, but it seems possible, even probable, that this Thanksgiving weekend will be the longest four days of his life.

"It's all over with Paula?" Julia doesn't sound sorry or not sorry; she sounds as if she's simply counting places at the table.

"Yeah. Things happen."

"Do you want to tell me more about it?"

"Nothing to tell."

After his first wife, the terrible Claudine, Lionel had thought he would never even sleep with another woman, but Paula had been the anti-Claudine: not French, not thin, not mean. She was plump and pretty, a good-natured woman with an English-language bookstore and a three-year-old son. It did not seem possible, when they married in the garden of the Hôtel des Saints-Pères, with Paula in a short white dress and her little boy holding the rings, that after five years she would be thin and irritable and given to the same shrugs and expensive cigarettes as the terrible Claudine. After he moved out, Lionel insisted on weekly dinners and movie nights with his stepson. He wants to do right by the one child to whom he is "Papa," although he has begun to think, as Ari turns eight, that there is no reason not to have the boy call him by his first name instead.

"Really nothing to tell. We were in love and then not."

"You slept with someone else?" Julia asks.

"Julia."

"I'm just trying to see how you got to 'not.' "

"I bet Buster told you."

"Your brother did not rat on you." He had, of course. Buster, the family big-mouth, a convert to monogamy, had told his mother that Lionel slept with the ticket taker from the cinema Studio 28, and Julia was not as shocked as Buster had hoped she would be. "A cutie, I bet," was all she said. (The beauty of Lionel's girlfriends was legendary. Paula, dimpled, fair, and curvy in her high heels, would have been the belle of any American country club, and even so was barely on the bottom rung of Lionel's girls.)

Buster talks about everything: his wife's dissolving sense of self, Jordan's occasional bed-wetting, Corinne's thumb-sucking, all just to open the door for his own concerns and sore spots—his climbing weight, his anxiety about becoming a judge so young. Julia thinks that Buster is a good and fine-looking man, and tall enough to carry the weight well, although it breaks her heart to see her boy so encumbered. She knows that he will make a fine judge, short on oratory and long on common sense and kindness.

"Even in my day, honey, most people got divorced because they had someone else on the side and got tired of pretending they didn't." Julia herself had been Lionel senior's someone on the side before she became his wife.

"Let's not go there. Anyway, definitely over with Paula. But I'm going to bring Ari every Thanksgiving."

Everyone had liked Paula (even when she got so crabby, it was not with the new in-laws three thousand miles away), but no one, including Lionel, can look at the poor kid without wanting to run a thumb up his slack spine. Bringing Ari is no gift to anyone; he's a burden to Jordan, an annoyance to little Corinne. Of course, Buster doesn't mind; he's the soft touch in the family, and Jewelle, inclined to love everything even faintly Buster, tries, but her whole beautiful frowning face signals that this is an inferior sort of child, one who does not appreciate friendly jokes or good cooking or the chance to ingratiate himself with his American family. It is to Ari's credit, Lionel thinks, that instead of clinging forlornly, he has retreated into bitter, silent, superior Frenchness.

"Julia, are you listening?" Lionel asks. "On Friday I'll fix the kitchen steps."

Julia sets down a platter of cold chicken and sits on the floor to do Colorforms with Jordan. She puts a red square next to Jordy's little green dots.

"It's like talking to myself. It's like I'm not even in the room." Lionel pours himself a drink, walking over to his nephew. Jordan peels a blue triangle off the bottom of Lionel's sneaker without looking up. Jordan takes after his father, and they both hate disturbances; Uncle Lionel can be a disturbance of the worst kind, the kind that might make Grandma Julia walk out of the room or put away the toys, slamming the cabinet door shut, knocking the hidden chocolates out of their boxes.

"Oh, we know you're here," Julia says. "We can tell because

your size thirteens are splayed all over Jordy's Colorforms. Squashing them."

"They're already flat, Julia," Lionel says, and she laughs. Lionel makes her laugh.

Jordan moves his Colorforms board a safe distance from his uncle's feet. Uncle Lionel is sharp, is what Jordan's parents say. Sharp as a knife. Ari, not really Uncle Lionel's son, not really Jordan's cousin, is sharp, too, but he's sharp mostly in French, so Jordan doesn't even have to get into it with him. Ari has Tintin and Jordan has Spider-Man, and Jordan stretches out on the blue velvet couch and Ari gets just the blue-striped armchair, plus Jordan has his own room and Ari has to share with Uncle Lionel.

"You invite Ari to play with you," Julia tells Jordan. "Take your sister with you."

"He's mean. And he only talks French, anyway. He's—"

"Jordy, invite your cousin to play with you. He's never been to America before, and you are the host."

"I'm the host?" Jordan can see himself in his blue blazer with his feet up on the coffee table like Uncle Lionel, waving a fat cigar.

"You are."

"All right. We're gonna play outside, then." Ari is not an outside person.

"That's nice," Lionel says.

"Nice enough," Julia says. It is terrible to prefer one grandchild over another, but who would not prefer sweet Jordan or Princess Corinne to poor long-nosed Ari, slinking around the house like a marmoset.

Julia has not had both sons with her for Thanksgiving for more than twenty years. Until 1978 the Sampson family sat around a big bird with corn-bread stuffing, pralined sweet potatoes, and three kinds of deep-dish pie, and it has been easier since her husband and in-laws died to stay in with a bourbon and a bowl of pasta when one son couldn't come home and the other didn't, and not too hard, later, to come as a pitied favorite guest to Buster's in-laws', and sweet and very easy, during the five happy, private years with Peaches Figueroa, for the two of them to wear their pajamas and eat fettuccine al barese in honor of Julia's Italian roots and in honor of Peaches, who had grown up with canned food and Thanksgiving from United Catholic Charities. With her whole extant family in the house now, sons and affectionate daughter-in-law (Jewelle must have had to promise her mother a hundred future Christmases to get away on Thanksgiving), grandson, granddaughter, and poor Ari, Lionel's little ex–step marmoset, Julia can see that she has entered Official Grandmahood. Sweet or sour, spry or arthritic, she is now a stock character, as essential and unknown as the maid in a drawing-room comedy.

"Looks good. Ari likes chicken." Lionel walks toward the sideboard.

Julia watches him sideways, his clever, darkly mournful eyes, the small blue circles of fatigue beneath them, the sparks of silver in his black curls. She does not say, How did we cripple you so? Don't some people survive a bad mother and her early death? Couldn't you have been the kind of man who overcomes terrible misfortune, even a truly calamitous error in judgment? It was just one night—not that that excuses anything, Julia thinks. She loves him like no one else; she remembers meeting him for the first time, wooing him for his father's sake and loving him exuberantly, openhandedly, without any of the prickling maternal guilt or profound irritation she sometimes felt with Buster. Just one shameful, gold-rimmed night together, and it still runs through her like bad sap. She has no idea what runs through him.

There is a knot in his heart, Julia thinks, as she puts away the Colorforms, and nothing will loosen it. She sees a line of ex–daughters-in-law, short and tall, dark and fair, stretching from Paris to Massachusetts, throwing their wedding bands into the sea and waving regretfully in her direction.

Julia kisses Lionel firmly on the forehead, and he smiles. It would be nicer if his stepmother's rare kisses and pats on the cheek did not feel so much like forgiveness, like Julia's wish to convey that she does not blame him for being who he is. Lionel wonders whom exactly she does blame.

"Let's talk later," he says. It seems safe to assume that later will not happen.

Lionel watches his niece and his sister-in-law through the kitchen door. He likes Jewelle. He always has. Likes her for loving his little brother and shaking him up, and likes her more now that she has somehow shaped Buster into a grown man, easy in his young family and smoothly armored for the outside world. He likes her for always making him feel that what she finds attractive in her husband she finds attractive, too, in the older, slightly darker brother-in-law. And Lionel likes, can't help being glad to see on his worst days, those spectacular breasts of hers, which, even as she has settled down into family life, no longer throwing plates in annoyance or driving to Mexico out of pique, she displays with the transparent pride of her youth.

"Looking good, Jewelle. Looking babe-a-licious, Miss Corinne."

They both smile, and Jewelle shakes her head. Why do the bad ones always look so good? Buster is a handsome man, but Lionel is just the devil.

"Are you here to help or to bother us?"

"Helping. He's helping me," Corinne says. She likes Uncle Lionel. She likes his big white smile and the gold band of his cigar, which he always, always gives to her, and the way he butters her bread, covering the slice right to the crust with twice as much butter as her mother puts on.

"I could help," Lionel says. There is an unopened bottle of Scotch under the sink, and he finds Julia's handsome, square, heavy-bottomed glasses, the kind that make you glad you drink hard liquor.

Lionel rolls up his sleeves and chops apples and celery. After Corinne yawns twice and almost tips over into the pan of cooling corn bread, Jewelle carries her off to bed. When she comes back from arranging Floradora the Dog and Strawberry Mouse just so, and tucking the blankets tightly around Corinne's feet, Lionel is gone, as Jewelle expected.

Her mother-in-law talks tough about men. Everything about Julia, her uniform of old jeans and black T-shirt, her wild gray hair and careless independence, says nothing is easier than finding a man and training him and kicking him loose if he doesn't behave, and you would think she'd raised both her boys as feminist heroes. And Buster is good—Jewelle always says so—he picks up after himself, cooks when he can, gives the kids their baths, and is happy to sit in the Mommy row during Jordan's Saturday swim. Lionel is something else. When he clears the table or washes up, swaying to Otis Redding, snapping his dish towel like James Brown, Julia watches him with such tender admiration that you would think he'd just rescued a lost child.

Jewelle runs her hands through the corn bread, making tracks in the crust, rubbing the big crumbs between her fingers. Julia's house, even with Lionel in it, is one of Jewelle's favorite places. At home, she is the Mommy and the Wife. Here, she is the mother of gifted children, an esteemed artist temporarily on leave. At her parents' house, paralyzed by habit, she drinks milk out of the carton, trying to rub her lipstick off the spout afterward, borrows her mother's expensive mascara and then takes it home after pretending to help her mother search all three bathrooms before they leave. She eats too much and too fast, half of it standing up and the rest with great reluctance, as if there were a gun pointed at her three times a day. In Julia's house there's no trouble about food or mealtimes; Jewelle eats what she wants, and the children eat bananas and Cheerios and grilled cheese sandwiches served up without even an arching of an eyebrow. Julia is happy to have her daughter-in-law cook interesting dishes and willing to handle the basics when the children are hungry and not one adult is intrigued by the idea of cooking.

Buster will not hear of anything but the corn bread–and–bacon stuffing Grammy Ruth used to make, and Jewelle, who would eat bacon every day if she could, makes six pounds of it and leaves a dark, crisp pile on the counter, for snacking. Julia seems to claim nothing on Thanksgiving but the table setting. She's not fussy—she prides herself on her lack of fuss—but Julia is particular about her table, and it is not Jewelle or Buster who is called on to pick up the centerpiece in town, but Lionel, who has had his license suspended at least two times that Jewelle knows of. Jewelle packs the stuffing into Tupperware and leaves a long note for Julia so that her mother-in-law will not think that she has abdicated on the sweet potatoes or the creamed spinach.

In bed, spooning Buster, Jewelle runs her hand down his warm back. Sweetness, she thinks, and kisses him between the shoulders. Buster throws one big arm behind him and pulls her close. Lucky Jewelle, lucky Buster. If Jewelle had looked out the window, she would have seen Lionel and Julia by the tire swing, talking the way they have since they resumed talking, casual and ironic, and beneath that very, very careful.

Lionel cradles the bottle of Glenlivet.

"You drink a lot these days," Julia says in the neutral voice she began cultivating twenty years ago, when it became clear that Lionel would never come back from Paris, would improve his French, graduate from L'Institut de Droit Comparé, and make his grown-up life anywhere but near her.

Lionel smiles. "It's not your fault. Blame the genes, Ma. Junkie mother, alcoholic dad. You did your best."

"It doesn't interfere with your work?" It's not clear even to Julia what she wants: Lionel unemployed and cadging loans from her, or drinking discreetly, so good at what he does that no one cares what happens after office hours.

"I am *so* good at my job. I am probably the best fucking

maritime lawyer in France. If you kept up with French news, you'd see me in the papers sometimes. Good and good-looking. And modest."

"I know you must be very good at your work. You can be proud of what you do. Pop would have been very proud of you."

Lionel takes a quick swallow and offers the bottle to Julia, and if it were not so clear to her that he is mocking himself more than her, that he wishes to spare her the trouble of worrying by showing just how bad it already is, she would knock the bottle out of his hand.

Lionel says, "I know. And you? What are you doing lately that you take pride in?"

Julia answers as if it's a pleasant question, the kind of fond interest one hopes one's children will show.

"I finished another book of essays, the piano in jazz. It's all right. It'll probably sell dozens, like the last one. You make sure to buy a few. I'm still gardening, not that you can tell this time of year."

"Buster says you're seeing someone."

"You have to watch out for Buster." Julia turns away. "Well, 'seeing.' It's Peter, my neighbor down the road. We like each other. His wife died three years ago."

"No real obstacles, then."

"Nope."

"How old is he? White or black?"

"He's a little older than me. White. You'll meet him tomorrow. I didn't want him to be alone. His daughter's in Baltimore this year with her husband's family."

"That's nice of you. Your first all-family Thanksgiving in twenty years—might as well have a few strangers to grease the wheels."

"It is nice, and he's only one person, and he is not a stranger to me or to Buster and Jewelle," Julia says, and walks into the house, thinking that it's too late in her personal day for talking to Lionel, that if she were driving she would have pulled off the road half an hour ago.

Julia starts cooking at six A.M. Early Thanksgiving morning is the only time she will have to herself. The rest of the day will be a joy, most likely, and so tiring that when Buster and Jewelle leave on Friday, right after Corinne is wrapped up in her car seat and Jordan squirms around for one last good-bye and their new car crunches down the gravel driveway, Julia will lie down with a cup of tea and not get up until the next day, when she will say good-bye to Lionel and Ari and lie down again. She reads Jewelle's detailed note and thinks, Poor Jewelle must be thirty-one—it's probably time for her to have Thanksgiving in her own house. Julia had to wrestle the holiday out of her own mother's hands; even as the woman lay dying she whispered directions for gravy and pumpkin pie, creating a chain of panicked, resentful command from bedroom to kitchen, with her daughter and two sisters slicing and basting to beat back the inevitable. Julia managed to celebrate one whole independent Thanksgiving, with four other newly hatched adults, only to marry Lionel senior the next summer and find the holiday permanently ensconced, like a small museum's only Rodin, at her new mother-in-law's house. Julia can sit now in her own kitchen, sixty years old with a dish towel in her hand, and hear Ruth Sampson saying to her, "My son is not cut from the same cloth as other people. You treat him right."

After this last, unexpected hurrah, Julia will let go of Thanksgiving altogether. She'll arrive at Jewelle's house, or Jewelle's mother's house, at just the right time, and entertain the children, and bring her own excellent lemon meringue pies and extravagant flowers to match their tablecloths. If things go well, maybe she'll bring Peter, too. As Julia pictures Peter entering Buster's front hall by her side, the two of them with bags of presents and a box of butter tarts, she cuts a wide white scoop through the end of her forefinger. Blood flows so fast it pools on the cutting board and drips onto the counter before she has even realized what the pain is.

"Ma." Lionel is behind her with paper towels. He packs her finger until it's the size of a dinner roll and holds it up over her head. "You stay like that. Sit. And keep your hand up."

"You're up early. The Band-Aids are in my bathroom." Her fingertip is throbbing like a heart, and Julia keeps it aloft. It's been a long time since anyone has told her to do anything.

Her bathrobe always lies at the foot of the bed. There is always a pale-blue quilt, and both nightstands are covered with books and magazines and empty teacups. The room smells like her. Lionel takes the Band-Aids from under the sink: styling mousse, Neosporin ointment (which he also takes), aloe-vera gel, Northern Lights shampoo for silver hair, two bottles of Pepto-Bismol, a jar of vitamin C, zinc lozenges, and a small plastic box of silver bobby pins.

When he comes down, Julia is holding her finger up, still pointing to God, in the most compliant, sweetly mocking way.

"I hear and obey," she says.

"That'll be the fucking day."

Lionel slathers the antibiotic ointment over her finger, holding the flap of skin down, and wraps two Band-Aids around it. It must hurt like holy hell by now, but she doesn't say so. With her good hand, Julia pats his knee.

"I was going to make coffee," she says, "but I think you'll have to." And even after Jewelle and Buster get up for the kids' breakfast and exclaim over the finger and Jewelle prepares to run the show, Lionel stays by Julia, changing the red bandages every few hours, mocking her every move, helping her with each dish and glass as if he were some fairy-tale combination of servant and prince.

At one o'clock, after Peter has called to say that he is too sick to come and everyone in the kitchen hears him coughing over the phone, they all go upstairs to change. They are not a dress-up family (another thing Jewelle likes, although she can hear her mother's voice suggesting that if one so disdains the holiday's traditions, why celebrate it at all), but the children are in such splendid once-a-year finery that it seems ungracious not to make an effort. Corinne wears a bronze organdy dress tied with a bronze satin sash, and ivory anklets and ivory Mary Janes. Julia knows this is nothing but nonsense and conspicuous consumption, but she loves the look of this little girl, right down to the twin bronze satin roses in her black hair, and she hopes she will remember it when Corinne comes to the dinner table ten years from now with a safety pin in her cheek or a leopard tattooed on her forehead. And Jordan is in his snappy fawn vest and white button-down shirt tucked into his navy-blue pants, and an adorable navy-blue-and-white-striped bow tie. Lionel and Buster are deeply dapper; their father appreciated Italian silks and French cotton, took his boys to Brooks Brothers in good times and Filene's Basement when necessary, and made buying a handsome tie as much a part of being a man as carrying a rubber or catching a ball, and they have both held on to that. Jewelle has the face and the figure to look good in almost everything, but Julia herself would not have chosen tight black satin pants, a turquoise silk camisole cut low, and a black satin jacket covered with bits of turquoise and silver, an unlikely mix of Santa Fe and disco fever. Julia comes downstairs in her usual holiday gray flannel pants and white silk shirt. She has turned her bathroom mirror, her hairbrushes, and her jewelry box over to Jewelle and Corinne.

"Do you mind Peter's not coming?" Buster says.

"Not really."

Lionel looks at her. "You must miss Pop," he says.

"Of course, honey. I miss him all the time." This is not entirely true. Julia misses Lionel senior when she hears an alto sax playing anything, even one weak note, and she misses him when she takes out the garbage; she misses him when she sees a couple dancing, and she misses him every time she looks at Buster, who has resembled her for most of his life, with his father apparent only in his curly hair, and now looks almost too much like the man she married.

Buster puts his arm around her waist. "You must miss Peaches, too." He'd met Peaches only a few times when she was well and charming, and a few more when she was dying, collapsed in his mother's bed like some great gray beast, all bones and crushed skin, barely able to squeeze her famous voice out through the cords.

Julia would like to say that missing Peaches doesn't cover it. She misses Peaches as much as she missed her stepson during his fifteen-year absence. She misses Peaches the way you miss good health when you have cancer. She misses her husband—of course she misses him and their twelve years together—but that grief has been softened, sweetened by all the time and life that came after. The wound of Peaches's death has not healed or closed up yet; at most the edges harden some as the days pass. She opens her mouth now to say nothing at all about her last love; she thinks that even if Lionel is all wrong about what kind of man Peter is, he is fundamentally right. Peter is not worth the effort.

"I do miss Peaches, too, of course."

Lionel has all of Peaches Figueroa's albums. On the first one, dark-blond hair waves around a wide bronze face, one smooth lock half covering a round green eye heavily made up. Black velvet wraps low across her breasts, and when Lionel was nineteen it was one of the small pleasures of his life to look at the dark-amber crescent of her aureole, just visible above the velvet rim, and listen to that golden, spilling voice.

"I'm sorry I didn't meet her." Lionel would like to ask his mother what it was like to go from a man to a woman, whether it changed Julia somehow (which he believes but cannot explain), and how she could go from his father and Peaches Figueroa, both geniuses of a kind, to Peter down the road, who sounds to Lionel like the most fatiguing, sorry-assed, ready-for-the-nursing home, limp-dick loser.

Julia raises an eyebrow and goes into the kitchen.

The men look at each other.

"We could open the wine," Lionel says. "You liked her, didn't you?"

"I really liked her," Buster says. He does not say, She scared the shit out of Jewelle, but she would have liked you, boy. She liked handsome, and she knew we all have that soft spot for talent, especially musical talent, and that we don't mind, we have even been known to encourage, a certain amount of accompanying attitude. Peaches had been Buster's favorite diva.

"Open the wine up. You let those babies breathe. I'll get everyone down here."

"It might be another half hour for the turkey," Jewelle says. "Sorry."

"Don't worry, honey." Buster eats one of Corinne's peanut-butter-stuffed celery sticks.

"Charades?" Julia says, putting out a small bowl of nuts and a larger one of black and green olives. Charades was their great family game, played in airports and hotel lobbies, played with very small gestures while flying to Denmark every summer for the Copenhagen jazz festival, played on Amtrak and in the occasional stretch limo to Newport, and played expertly by Lionel and Buster whenever the occasion has arisen since. Corinne and Jordan don't know what charades is, but Grandma Julia has already taken them back to the kitchen and distributed two salad bowls, six pencils, and a pile of scrap paper. Corinne will act out *The Cat in the Hat,* and Jordan will do his favorite song, "Miami." Corinne practices making the hat shape and stepping into it while Jordan pulls off his bow tie and slides on his knees across the kitchen floor, wild and shiny and fly like Will Smith. They are naturals, Julia thinks, and thinks further that it is a ridiculous thing to be pleased about—who knows what kind of people they will grow up to be?—but she cannot help believing that their mostly good genes and their ability to play charades are as reasonable an assurance of future success as anything else.

No one wants to be teamed with Jewelle. She is smart about many things, talented in a dozen ways, and an excellent mother, and both men think she looks terrific with the low cups of her turquoise lace top ducking in and out of view, but she's no good at charades. She goes blank after the first syllable and stamps her foot and blinks back tears until her time is up. She never gets the hard ones, and even with the easiest title she guesses blindly without listening to what she's said. Jewelle is famous for "Exobus" and "Casabroomca."

I can't put husband and wife together, Julia thinks, feeling the tug of dinner-party rules she has ignored for twenty years. "Girls against boys, everybody?"

Jewelle claims the couch for the three girls, and Buster and Lionel look at each other. It is one of the things they like best about their mother; she would rather be kind than win. They slap hands. Unless Corinne is very, very good in a way that is not normal for a three-year-old, they will wipe the floor with the girl team.

Jewelle is delighted. Julia is an excellent guesser and a patient performer.

Lionel says, "Rules, everybody." No one expects the children to do anything except act out their charades and yell out meaningless guesses. The recitation of rules is for Jewelle. "No talking while acting. Not even whispering. No foreign languages—"

"Not even French," Jewelle says. Lionel is annoying in English; he is obnoxious in French.

"Not even French. No props. No mouthing. Kids, look." He shows them the signs for book and television and movie and musical, for little words, for "sounds like."

Jordan says, "Where's Ari?"

They all look around the room. Jewelle sighs. "Jordy, go get him. He's probably still in Uncle Lionel's room. When did you see him last, Lionel?" she says.

Jordan runs up the stairs.

"I didn't lose him, Jewelle. He's probably just resting. It was a long trip."

Ari comes down in crumpled khakis and a brown sweater. Terrible colors for him, Jewelle and Julia think.

In French, Lionel says, "Good boy. You look ready for dinner. Come sit by me and I'll show you how to play this game."

Ari sits on the floor in front of his stepfather. He doesn't expect that the game will be explained to him; it will be in very fast English, it will make them all laugh with one another, and his stepfather, who is already winking at stupid baby Corinne, will go on laughing and joking, in English.

The children perform their charades, and the adults are almost embarrassed to be so pleased. As Julia stands up to do *Love's Labour's Lost,* Jewelle says, "Let me just run into the kitchen."

Lionel says, "Go ahead, Ma. You're no worse off with Corinne," and Buster laughs and looks at the floor. He loves Jewelle, but there is something about this particular disability that seems so harmlessly funny; if she were fat, or a bad dancer, or not very bright, he would not laugh, ever.

As Julia is very slowly helping Corinne guess that it's three words, Jewelle walks into the living room, struggling with the large turkey still sizzling on the wide silver platter.

"It's that time," she says.

Buster says, "I'll carve," and Jewelle, who heard him laugh, says, "No, Lionel's neater—let him do it."

They never finish the charades game. Corinne and Jordan and Ari collapse on the floor after dinner, socks and shoes scattered, one of Corinne's bronze roses askew, the other in Ari's sneaker. Ari and Jordan have dismantled the couch. Jewelle and Buster gather the three of them, wash their faces, drop them into pajamas, and put them to bed. They kiss their beautiful, damp children, who smell of soap and corn bread and lemon meringue, and they kiss Ari, who smells just like his cousins.

Buster says, "Do we have to go back down?"

"Are you okay?" Jewelle rubs his neck.

"Just stuffed. And I'm ready to be with just you." Buster looks at his watch. "Lionel's long knives ought to be coming out around now."

"Do you think we ought to hang around for your mother?"

"To protect her? I know you must be kidding."

It's all right with Jewelle if Buster thinks they've cleaned up enough; the plates are all in the kitchen, the leftover turkey has been wrapped and refrigerated, the candles have been blown out. It's not her house, after all.

Lionel washes, Julia dries. They've been doing it this way since he was ten, and just as he cannot imagine sleeping on the left side of a bed or wearing shoes without socks, he cannot imagine drying rather than washing. Julia looks more than tired; she looks maimed.

"If your hand's hurting, just leave the dishes. They'll dry in the rack."

Julia doesn't even answer. She keeps at it until clean, dry plates and silver cover the kitchen table.

"If you leave it until tomorrow, I'll put it all away," Lionel says.

Julia thinks that unless he really has become someone she does not know, everyone will have breakfast in the dining room, and afterward, sometime in the late afternoon, when Buster and his family have gone and it's just Lionel and Ari, when it would be nice to sit down with a glass of wine and watch the sun set, she will be putting away her mother's silver platter and her mother-in-law's pink-and-gold crystal bowls, which go with nothing but please the boys.

Lionel and Julia talk about Buster and Jewelle's marriage, which is better but less interesting than it was, and Buster's weight problem, and Jewelle's languishing career as a painter, and Odean

Pope's Saxophone Choir, and Lionel's becoming counsel for a Greek shipping line.

Lionel sighs over the sink, and Julia puts her hand on his back. "Are you all right? Basically?"

"I'm fine. You don't have to worry about me. I'm not a kid." He was about to say that he's not really a son, any more than he's really a father, that these step-ties are like long-distance relationships, workable only with people whose commitment and loyalty are much greater than the average. "And you don't have to keep worrying about . . . what was. It didn't ruin me. It's not like we would ever be lovers now."

Julia thinks that all that French polish is not worth much if he can't figure out a nicer way to say that he no longer desires her, that sex between them is unthinkable not because she raised him, taught him to dance, hemmed his pants, and put pimple cream on his back, but because she is too old now for him to see her that way.

"We were never lovers. We had sex," she says, but this is not what she believes. They were lovers that night as surely as ugly babies are still babies; they were lovers like any other mismatched and blundering pair. "We were heartbroken and we mistook each other for things we were not. Do you really want to have this conversation?"

Lionel wipes down the kitchen counters. "Nope. I have never wanted to have this conversation. I don't want anything except a little peace and quiet—and a Lexus. I'm easy, Ma."

Julia looks at him so long he smiles. He is such a handsome man. "You're easy. And I'm tired. You want to leave it at that?"

Lionel tosses the sponge into the sink. "Absolutely. Take care of your finger. Good night."

If it would turn him back into the boy he was, she would kiss him good night, even if she cut her lips on that fine, sharp face.

"Okay. See you in the morning. Sleep tight."

Julia takes a shower. Lionel drinks on in the kitchen, the Scotch back under the sink in case someone walks in on him. Buster and Jewelle sleep spoons-style. Corinne has crawled between them, her wet thumb on her father's bare hip, her small mouth open against her mother's shoulder. Jordan sleeps as he always does, wrestling in his dreams whatever he has failed to soothe and calm all day. His pillow is on the floor, and the sheets twist around his waist.

Julia reads until three A.M. Most nights she falls asleep with her arms around her pillow, remembering Peaches's creamy breasts cupped in her hands or feeling Peaches's soft stomach pressed against her, but tonight, spread out in her pajama top and panties, she can hardly remember that she ever shared a bed.

Ari is snuffling in the doorway.

"Come here, honey. *Viens ici, chéri.*" It is easier to be kind to him in French, somehow. Ari wears one of Buster's old terry-cloth robes, the hem trailing a good foot behind him. He has folded the sleeves back so many times they form huge baroque cuffs around his wrists.

"I do not sleep."

"That's understandable. *Je comprends.*" Julia pats the empty side of the bed, and Ari sits down. His doleful, cross face is handsome in profile, the bedside light limning his Roman nose and straight black brows.

"Jordan hate me. You all hate me."

"We don't hate you, honey. *Non, ce n'est pas vrai. Nous t'aimons.*" Julia hopes that she is saying what she means. "It's just hard. We all have to get used to each other. *Il faut que nous . . .*" If she ever had the French vocabulary to discuss the vicissitudes of divorce and future happiness and loving new people, she doesn't anymore. She puts her hand on Ari's flat curls. *"Il faut que nous fassions ta connaissance."*

She hears him laugh for the first time. "That is 'how do you do.' Not what we say *en famille.*"

Laughing is an improvement, and Julia keeps on with her

French—perhaps feeling superior will do him more good than obvious kindness—and tries to tell Ari about the day she has planned for them tomorrow, with a trip to the playground and a trip to the hardware store so Lionel can fix the kitchen steps.

Ari laughs again and yawns. "I am tired," he says, and lies down, putting his head on one of Julia's lace pillows. *"Dors bien,"* the little boy says.

"All right. You, too. You *dors bien.*"

Julia pulls the blankets up over Ari.

"At night my mother sing," he says.

The only French song Julia knows is "La Marseillaise." She sings the folk songs and hymns she sang to the boys, and by the time she has failed to hit that impossible note in "Amazing Grace," Ari's breathing is already moist and deep. Julia gets under the covers as Ari rolls over, his damp forehead and elbows and knees pressing into her side. She counts the books on her shelves, then sheep, then turns out the bedside lamp and counts every lover she ever had and everything she can remember about them, from the raven-shaped birthmark on the Harvard boy's shoulder to the unexpected dark brown of Peter's eyes, leaving out Peaches and Lionel senior, who are on their own, quite different list. She remembers the birthday parties she gave for Lionel and Buster, including the famous Cookie Monster cake that turned her hands blue for three days, and the eighth-grade soccer party that ended with Lionel and another boy needing stitches. Already six feet tall, he sat in her lap, arms and legs flowing over her, while his father held his head for the doctor.

Ari sighs and shifts, holding tight to Julia's pajama top, her lapel twisted in his hands like rope. She feels the wide shape of his five knuckles on her chest, bone pressing flesh against bone, and she is not sorry at all to be old and awake so late at night.

FORT USELESS AND FORT RIDICULOUS

Lionel Sampson reads to his brother from the flight magazine. " 'The Seeing Eye dog was invented by a blind American.' "

Buster laughs. "Really. *Invented.* Man must have gone through a hell of a lot of dogs."

Julia's sons, Buster and Lionel, are flying from Paris to Boston, to be picked up and driven to their mother's house for Thanksgiving. Their driver will be an old Russian guy they've had before, big belly, a few missing teeth, with cold bottled water and *The New York Times* in the backseat. The two men are as happy as clams not to be driving in Buster's wife's minivan with all the kids and their laptops and iPods and duffel bags and Jewelle's gallon containers of creamed spinach and mashed sweet potatoes, which Jewelle now brings rather than making them at her mother-in-law's, because now that Julia's getting on, although the house is clean and Jewelle is not saying it's *not* clean, you do have to tidy up a little before you get to work in Julia's kitchen, and Jewelle would just rather not.

Lionel closes the magazine and the homely flight attendant brings them water. (Remember when they were pretty? Lionel says. Remember when Pop took us to Denmark, Buster says, and they all wore white stockings and white miniskirts?) The flight attendant lays linen napkins in their laps. Lionel likes first class so much that even when a client doesn't pay for it, he pays for the upgrade himself, and he's paid for Buster's upgrade, too. Lionel spends more on travel than he does on rent. His wife thinks he's crazy. Patsine grew up riding the bumper of dusty Martinique buses and as far as she's concerned, even now, your own seat and no chickens is all that anyone needs.

Buster opens another magazine. "Looky here, little girl in northern India is born with two faces. Only one set of ears, but two full faces. She's worshipped in her village. Durga, goddess of valor."

"Jesus," Lionel says. "What's wrong with people?" He looks at the picture of the little girl. "Patsine's pregnant."

"Oh, great. Good for you. Patsine's great." Buster has disliked all of Lionel's other girlfriends and wives. The mean ones scared him and the nice, hopeful ones depressed him and Jewelle would say to him, after each meet-and-greet, "All I'm saying is, just once, let him bring someone who isn't a psycho, a slut, or a Martian. Just once." Buster pats his big brother on the knee and says, Well, aren't you the proud papa, and the homely flight attendant smiles at them both. *Mes félicitations, monsieur.* She brings them pâté and crackers and two flutes of Champagne. Lionel gives his Champagne to Buster and asks for sparkling water.

Buster keeps reading. "It says the village chief wants the government to build a temple to the two-faced baby."

"Who wouldn't," Lionel says.

They're over the north Atlantic, only ten hours until home and eating a pretty good lunch, as Buster is not one to say no to a good meal. Buster sips his Champagne and Lionel drinks his Perrier and stifles his envy and longing by reviewing all the terrible things that happened to him when he was drinking. He nearly killed an old lady on a Sunday drive; he fell down a flight of stairs and ripped open his scalp, so that when he sat in court the next day, the judge finally said, M. Sampson, the blood is distracting me, and Lionel left to tighten his bandage and came back to a trail of red drops at his side of the table. He lost the case and the goodwill of his partners. If you want to look at the big picture, as Lionel tries to these days—his drinking has led to failed relationships with women who had nothing in common except bad judgment and despair.

As her husband and brother-in-law are over the north Atlantic, Jewelle piles all of her children's things into the van and Jordan and her nephew Ari play basketball and Patsine makes several slow, steady trips to the van, each time carrying something small and not too heavy. Corinne doesn't help even that much, because she's taken off to her best friend's house, so she and the other girl can weep and embrace as if the Thanksgiving weekend apart is a life sentence. Jewelle can't say a thing to her daughter about her drama-queen behavior or her aggrieved and enormous uselessness because they have just gotten over a huge blowup about people of color, a category in which Jewelle Enright Sampson (English, Irish, and Belgian) does not figure, but her daughter, Corinne Elizabeth Sampson, does. (I joined the NMS Students of Color group, Corinne told her family, after her first day of middle school. I'm secretary. No one said, What color is that? And no one pointed out that Corinne was a few shades lighter than even the all-white people in the family. Her brother, Jordan, who is more coffee-with-a-lot-of-cream, snickered, and her father, who is a brown-skinned man, shook his head fondly. Jewelle called her mother-in-law, the only other white mother of tan children whom she knew, and complained. Julia told her that white mothers of black children were screwed whichever way they went: white trash or in denial or so supportive, they're punch lines for black *and* white people, filling their shopping carts with Rastafarian lip balm and Jheri curl products and both kinds of Barbie dolls. Someone's got to be the mammy, she said to Jewelle; unfortunately, it's our turn. Think Halle Berry, she said; she seems to like her mother.)

When everyone is safely in the van, Jewelle wants to discuss the visit to Julia's. I'm not *criticizing,* she says. I didn't say the kitchen *isn't* clean, she says to Patsine. Patsine has visited their mother-in-law only once before and the kitchen was neither dirty nor clean; it was unexceptional and she doesn't care. Patsine says to Jewelle, You must forgive me, I am completely exhausted, and she closes her eyes. Corinne sits between her brother and her cousin and she is very aware of her cousin Ari's long thigh pressing against hers, of his fidgeting from time to time, of his bare arm across her shoulders. All the children are listening to their music and Patsine is sleeping, or pretending to sleep, and Jewelle just drives to the Cape.

As the Russian guy is waiting for Buster and Lionel, as Jewelle is driving everyone to the Cape, Julia and her dog, Sophie Tucker, and her friend Robert lie in bed.

"Everyone is coming home later," Julia says.

"So you've said. I won't leave a trace."

Robert gets out of bed and stands in front of the window, looking out at the ocean. The soft light falls over him, over his big shoulders and thick torso and thick legs, everything just faintly webbed by age except his impossibly bright gold hair.

"I don't suppose you'd like to come to dinner," Julia says. "You could bring Arthur."

Robert shakes his head and gets back into bed. Julia tucks two pillows under his knees to protect his back.

"Oh, darling, could you . . ." he says.

"Oh, darling yourself," Julia says and gets him another glass of cold water.

"You're too good to me. Let's get facials Saturday. On me."

"I could use one," Julia says, and she thinks that she could more than use one, that when she stopped coloring her hair, she just let the whole edifice collapse, from roof to rail, except for long walks with the dog.

Robert put his hands at his temples and pulls. He says "Honey, who couldn't use one? I myself am going to start taping my eyebrows to my hairline like Lucille Ball."

"Okay," Julia says. "Me, too." She rests her head on his shoulder and Robert strokes her hair, tucking a few strands behind her ear. "You won't come?"

"No," Robert says. "We can't. You have nice ears."

"They've held up."

"They have held up *wonderfully,*" he says, and he pulls the quilt up over Julia's bare shoulder and begins snoring.

A few hours later, Robert goes home to his lover, Arthur, who looks at Robert over his newspaper and sighs. Julia puts on her raincoat and takes Sophie Tucker for a walk.

Robert is sitting at the kitchen table, waiting for Julia's family to come. He's been there all morning. He hears the car coming up the drive and goes to the porch. Jordan sees him first.

"It's the old man," he says, and Jewelle peers forward.

Robert taps on the van window and helps Patsine out of the van. He's very strong for an old man. Jewelle moves too quickly for him to open the door for her and she feels a little slighted that he doesn't, and as she is thinking that her mother-in-law must have fallen asleep on the couch, Robert pulls the two women toward the side of the porch, toward the browning hydrangeas. He tells them that Julia is dead.

He tells them everything he knows about the accident, which is only what the police told him when he had come back to the house for tea and found no Julia, and there was blood on the road and Sophie Tucker whimpering on the porch. Robert carried Sophie Tucker inside and the two policemen said it was a terrible accident, they said no alcohol was involved, they said the boy told them the dog ran across the street and Julia ran after it, and in the wet weather, the boy lost control of the car. The boy was in the hospital, the police said, and Julia was dead.

Robert hugs each of the women and Corinne runs over, like a little girl in a bad thunderstorm, to push her way under her mother's arm. Patsine wishes her husband were here now to tell Ari, this boy she hardly knows, that his grandmother, whom she hardly knows, is dead. She tells Ari, in French, what has happened and he looks at her, stone-faced, and goes to his room in the attic. Jordan presses himself to Jewelle's other side and he finds Corinne's hand. Jewelle kisses both of them, frantically, and says, Oh, I'm sorry, honey, your nana is just so sorry not to be here.

Jewelle and her children go into the house and upstairs like one person. Robert offers Patsine his arm and the two of them stand in the front hall, until Robert says that perhaps he ought to go home and Patsine agrees.

When Buster and Lionel arrive, pulling their bags out of the trunk, Jewelle and Patsine run out to meet them on the driveway and the two men back away, a little, before their wives even speak. Lionel drops to his knees on the lawn and Buster kneels beside him and the two women sit down beside them, all of them on the damp, crisp grass as the driver pulls away. The four of them unload Jewelle's van and Lionel and Buster go from room to room, kissing the children good night. In the morning, they find Ari in his grandmother's bed.

"Is anyone going to the store?" Lionel yells up the stairs, and no one answers. Jewelle is walking on the beach. Patsine is napping. Jordan lies on one of the twin beds in the attic room, looking at a few old copies of *Playboy* his father or his uncle must have left behind. Corinne has taken over the living room, her dirty sneakers and sweaters trailing over the sofa and a gold-framed photograph of her latest hero, Damien de Veuster, dead leper priest, on the coffee table. It's Jordan who has the right disposition for yoga, Lionel thinks; the boy's a limpid pool of goodness in a family of undertow, and Lionel doesn't know where he gets it. (Julia would have said that Jordan was very like Lionel's father's father, Alfred Sampson, who even as a black man in Worcester, Massachusetts, in 1963, and even among white people hoping the world would never change, was revered throughout the town, and when he died, Irish cops sent flowers.) But Jordan is in the attic with his door locked and here instead is Corinne, a big-busted, wild-haired girl, her bodhichitta tank top rising over her round, tan belly, her green stretch pants dipping very close to her ass crack, racing toward enlightenment and altruism like the Cannonball Express.

"You wanna take the bike to the grocery, Corinne?" Lionel asks.

Corinne puts a finger to her lips, as if her uncle Lionel is disturbing not her, *which wouldn't matter in the least,* but the tranquillity of her spiritual guides. She exhales deeply and squeezes her eyes closed.

"Christ almighty." Lionel yells upstairs. "Is anyone going to the goddamned store before it closes?"

Lionel can't go; he doesn't have a license. France—his home for some thirty years and a nation exceptionally tolerant of drinking and driving—lowered the blood-alcohol level to something like a glass of water with a splash of Pernod and now he can't drive anywhere, not legally. He doesn't try. Not driving is his penance, like not drinking, which is itself so preoccupying and gives him such a novel and peculiar and fraught perspective on every activity, he could almost say he doesn't mind, although he has thought a lot about Balvenie Scotch in a heavy crystal glass for the last two days. Ari jumps down the stairs in two huge steps, punches his stepfather in the arm, and hangs in the doorway to watch Corinne breathe. He breathes with her for a moment. Late last summer, Corinne put her hand on his cock by accident when he spilled his juice and she went to help him mop it up and then she felt him and she dropped the roll of paper towels in his lap and went back to her seat, but that moment is what Ari has come back for.

Late last summer, when everyone had come to Julia's for Labor Day, Julia took them all into town for Italian ices. The eight of them sat on the wrought-iron benches in front of Vincenzo's, sucking on paper cups of lemon and tangerine. Julia stood up. She threw her paper cup to the ground and cupped her hands around her mouth. She yelled, "Robert. Robert Nash." And at the far end of the street, two men turned around and came toward her. Julia began to hurry toward the taller man, and he put his arms around her and all they could see was his crisp white shirtsleeves and gold watch, and when Julia stepped back and put her hand to his face, they saw his pressed jeans, his bare feet in Italian loafers. *"Très chic,"* Jewelle whispered. Julia and the old man hugged again and finally Julia introduced everyone. ("Oh, Robert, my son Lionel, my grandson Ari, my granddaughter, Corinne, my grandson Jordan, my son Buster—I'm so sorry, honey, I should say my son Judge Gabriel Sampson and his wife, Jewelle. How's that?") And the old man looked Lionel up and down in an unmistakable way. ("I'd know you anywhere," he said. "Your father's son.") He shook hands with everyone. He said, "It's a pleasure to meet you all. This is my companion, Arthur." The other man looked like a middle-aged hamster and he cradled a big bouquet from the florist, wrapped in lavender tissue and cellophane.

Jordan poked Ari and Ari rolled his eyes.

Robert said, "And what are you two young men doing for amusement?"

He didn't sound like an elegant old fruit; he sounded like a distinguished and rather demanding English professor, and Julia hid her smile when the boys dropped their eyes. Robert used to reduce college boys of all kinds, potheads, lacrosse players, and clean-cut Christians, to tears with that tone.

Ari shrugged. Conversation with American strangers was Jordan's department.

Jordan said, "We might do a little fishing."

"Fly-fishing?"

"No. Just, you know, regular," Jordan said.

Lionel nodded. "Just reel and rods and worms. Nothing fancy."

Robert smiled again. "Well, if you can handle a little motorboat, I have one just rusting in the driveway. You're welcome to it."

Everyone except Arthur smiled and Lionel could see the man calculating the cost of the lawsuit when one of the boys lost a hand in the propeller or came home crying after an afternoon skinny-dipping at Robert's.

Lionel put a protective arm around each boy and began to shift them away.

Robert said, "Well, come look at the boat if you want. And there's a basketball court across the street. My neighbor's in Greece and it just sits there. It's a waste."

"We could ride over tomorrow," Jordan said

"C'est de la balle." Ari glanced toward the old man. "Cool."

"Just as you say. Arthur, do show them where we are," Robert said, and Arthur handed each of the boys a business card with Robert's name and phone number and a little pen-and-ink map on the back, marking their house with a silver star.

Robert said to Julia, "And you must have these," and he took the huge bunch of pink and yellow alstroemeria from Arthur, flowers they'd gotten for their front hall, and handed them to Julia. She kissed him again and ducked her head into the flowers, sniffing, although there was no real scent, and she exclaimed, like a girl, all the way home.

Lionel and Julia walked behind the others.

"You think the boys should go over there?"

Julia turned on him. "He's an old friend of mine, Lionel. He was a friend of your father's and he was extending himself, out of kindness, to my *grandchildren.*" And Lionel was glad he didn't say what he was thinking.

Finally, someone does go to the grocery store and people sit, in knots of two or three, on the deck, or walk on the beach or walk in and out of Julia's room. Lionel and Buster smoke on the front porch. Someone orders in bad pizza and they eat it off paper plates and even Jewelle does nothing more in the kitchen than dump the cold slices in a pile and refrigerate them. By ten o'clock, Buster and Jewelle are listening to Lionel and Patsine in the next room. Lionel is talking angrily and Patsine makes a soft, soothing sound. Then Lionel gets up and goes down the hall for a glass of water and they can hear everything, even the click of the bedroom door as Lionel closes it. Patsine asks a question and Lionel gets back into bed and then there is more whispering and a little uncertain laughter and then Buster is glad he can't see Jewelle's face while his brother gets a blow job.

When Buster was fifteen and Lionel was twenty-five, Julia sent Buster to spend the summer with his brother in Paris. Buster spent his days riding the Métro, listening to music from home, and trying to pick up girls. At night, Lionel made dinner for them both.

"How's it goin'? With the ladies?"

Buster shrugged. Lionel poured them both a glass of wine.

"Listen to me," Lionel said, "and not to those assholes back home. You do not want to get advice from sixteen-year-old boys. You don't want to be the kind of guy who just grabs some tit or a handful of pussy and then goes and tells his friends so they can say, 'You da man.' "

"No," Buster said.

"That's right, no, you don't. You want to be the kind of man women beg for sex. You want women saying, 'Oh, yes, baby, yes, baby, yes' " and on the last "yes," he got up, took a peach from a bowl on the counter, and sliced it in half. He threw the pit into the wastebasket and he put the fruit, shiny side up, in Buster's hand.

"Here you go. See that little pink point. You got to lick that little point, rub your tongue over and around it." He smacked Buster on the back of the head. "Don't slobber. You're not a washcloth. You. Are. A. Lover."

Buster breathed in peach smell and he flicked his tongue at the tiny point.

"That's it, that's what I'm talking about. Lick it. It won't bite you, boy. Lick it again. Now, you get in there with your nose and your chin."

"My nose," Buster said, and Lionel pressed the tip of Buster's nose into the peach.

"Your nose, your chin. Your forehead, if that's what it takes."

Buster gave himself to the peach until there was nothing but exhausted peach skin and bits of yellow fruit clinging to his face.

Lionel handed him a dish towel.

"How long do you do it for?" Buster asked.

"How long? Until her legs are so tight around your head you can't actually hear the words but you know she's saying, Don't stop, don't stop, oh, my God in heaven, don't you stop."

"And then what?" Buster picked up another peach, just in case.

"And you keep on. And then she comes. Unless. Unless, you're slurping away down there for ten minutes and nothing's happening, you know, and all of a sudden she arches her back like this"—and Lionel arched his back, until his head was almost to the floor—"and she yells, Oh, Jesus, I'm coming." Lionel screamed. And then said, "If that happens, she's faking."

Buster almost choked on this, the thought that he would practice all summer, become as good a lover as his brother, and then the girl would only be pretending to like it?

"Oh, why would she do that?"

Lionel shrugged. "Because she doesn't want to embarrass your sorry ass and she also doesn't want to lie there all night, waiting for nothing."

"That happens?"

Lionel poured them both another glass. "Oh, yes. Sometimes you do your best, and it's not good enough. So you man up, limp dick, shattered spirit. You pick yourself up and you say to her, Tell me what you really want. You say to her, Put your little hand where you want mine to be." Lionel drains his glass. "And you do like she shows you. Don't worry—the ladies are going to love you, Buster."

And Buster wraps his arm around his wife's soft waist, beneath her nightgown, and she pulls it up and places his hand on her breast. Their dance is Buster's palm settling over her nipple, his fingertips sliding up the side of her breast, Jewelle rolling over to put her face next to Buster's, Jewelle licking at the creases in Buster's neck. Jewelle runs her hand along the smooth underside of his belly and he sighs.

"Oh, you feel so good," she says. "You always do."

"My Jewelle," he says.

"Oh, yes," she says. "No one else's."

They love this old dance.

"I think we should do it right away. We're all here." Jewelle has waited for Lionel to speak but he's been lying on the couch for ten minutes, not saying a word.

"What is the 'it'?" Patsine asks.

Jewelle looks at Patsine. Patsine has something pointed and sensible to say about everything, all the time.

"I think the 'it' is a memorial service."

Lionel lifts his head a bit, so he can see everyone.

"I hope that little sonofabitch dies," he says, and he sits up, changing his tone. "You know, her wishes were very clear. Cremation and lunch. No clergy, no house of worship, and no big deal. Obit in the *Cranberry Bog Times* or whatever and that's it."

"Cremation?" Patsine asks, and shrugs when everyone looks at her. Julia was not her mother and it's not her business but she liked Julia very much and she would not slide a beloved into the mouth of a furnace by way of farewell.

"Why not? It's not like she was Jewish," Corinne says. It really isn't Patsine's place to ask all of these questions when she's been married to Uncle Lionel for about five minutes.

"Her father was Jewish," Lionel says, and everyone looks at him.

"Her father was Jewish? Julia was half Jewish?" Jewelle says.

"Well, not the side that counts," Lionel says.

"I'm part Jewish?" Corinne says.

"Yes," Lionel says. "You are not only a quadroon, you are also, fractionally, a Jewess. You can be blackballed by *everyone*."

Buster puts his hand on Corinne's shoulder and shakes his head at his brother.

"Nice."

Lionel lies back down. He recites.

"Ma's mother was Italian. Her father was Jewish. We never met either of them. The old man ran off and left them when Ma was a girl and her mother raised her nothing, which is why we are the faithless heathen we are. Long after the divorce, the old man dies in a car accident—I think." He looks at Buster, in case he's gotten it wrong—it's thirty-five years since he heard the story—but Buster shrugs. He was even younger when Julia told them the story and it doesn't seem to him that he ever heard it again. Buster shrugs again, to show that he's already forgiven his brother for teasing Corinne. She needs it; his daughter has become like fucking Goebbels on the subject of race and he can't stand it. "He never remarried and he left all his money to Ma's mother. She went on a round-the-world cruise after Ma graduated college and then . . . she dies. That's all, folks." Lionel spreads his arms wide, like Al Jolson.

Patsine says flatly, "Jewish men do not abandon their wives."

Is that so, Jewelle thinks. She guesses some French Jewish married man sometime must have not left his wife for Miss Patsine Belfond, and Jewelle arches an eyebrow at Corinne. Lionel kisses Patsine's puffy ankle. He loves her politically incorrect and sensible assertions. Fat people do eat too much. Some people should be sterilized. The darker people's skins, the noisier they are, until you get to certain kinds of Africans who are as silent as sand.

"Well, apparently one did," Lionel says cheerfully. "Although Grandpa Whoever, Morris, Murray, Yitzhak, made up for it by leaving Grandma Whoever a lot of money, which was great until she died of food poisoning in Shanghai or—"

"Bangkok." Buster says. "Bhutan?"

"Burma?"

"She died of food poisoning?" Corinne says.

"Bad shrimp," Lionel says, closing his eyes.

He hears his brother say, "Or crab," and he smiles.

"People don't *die* from food poisoning," Corinne says.

Jewelle has had enough. "Your aunt Helen almost died from food poisoning when we were girls. We were at the state fair and she got so sick from the fried clams she was hospitalized for it. She vomited for three days and she was skinny as a stick anyway. She really almost died." Corinne and Jordan stare at their mother. Their aunt Helen is big and imperturbable, a tax lawyer who brings her own fancy wine and her own pillow when she visits, and it's impossible to imagine her young and skinny, barfing day and night until she almost died.

Lionel presses his feet against his wife's strong thigh and keeps his eyes shut. If he keeps them closed long enough, everyone but Patsine and Buster will disappear, his mother will reappear, and the worst headache he has ever had will go away.

"I guess there are always things people don't know about each other. I didn't know that about Helen and the clams." Buster takes out a pencil. "I think we should do a little planning, for the service, the lunch, for Ma."

"Fuck you," Lionel says.

"I know."

Robert has been standing in the doorway for about half a minute, listening to his friend's children. He wants to write it all down and tell Julia after. You wouldn't *believe* it, he'd say. They are all just like you said. Lionel is completely the master of the universe—you must have loved him a lot, darling, to give him that self-confidence—and Buster is Ted E. Bear on the outside but very strong on the inside; you'd sleep with Lionel but you'd marry Buster, is what I'm saying. Well, not you, of course, but me—back in the day. And poor Jewelle, doomed to be runner-up, isn't she, even with those absolutely fantastic tits and still workin' it, but my God, Patsine, what a piece of work. Don't ask her if that dress makes you look fat because she *will* tell you. But I can see why you were thrilled she married Lionel. She has bent that man to her will and he is so glad, I can tell you that. Jordan's a love; he's like Buster, although maybe without the brains. Julia would pretend to smack him and he would apologize and she would say, Go on, go on eviscerating my loved ones, you terrible man. And he'd say, Corinne, my God, that child is why convents were *invented*. And Ari is very sexy in that broody, miserable way but it's hard to see what exactly one would *do* with him. And Julia would look at him and he would say, I'm just sharing my observations, and she would say, You should be locked up, and he would say, And then you'd miss me, and she would say, Yes, I would, and I'd visit you in jail once a month and bring you porn.

Corinne sees Robert first and she pokes her uncle Lionel. They all look over at Robert and they all say hello, more or less.

"Would you like a cup of coffee?" Jewelle says.

"No, thank you. I'm sorry to disturb you. I just thought I would . . . come by."

"We're planning a service, just a lunch," Lionel says, and Robert can see how hard the man is trying to be civil. "Maybe you want to say a few words."

"Yes," Robert says to the roomful of people who don't want him there. He is an impediment; he is an awful, faggy roadblock to their mother's memory, and the sooner he picks up his odds and ends and goes back to Old Fagland, the better. Robert is not a brave man; he has stood up for himself a couple of times, in a polite way, over the course of seventy years, but he isn't the kind of person who stays where he isn't wanted. Julia was. Julia was just that kind of person, going where she wasn't wanted, telling people to go fuck themselves, and Julia had loved him. He had braided her long gray hair and they had discussed whether or not she should cut it after all this time, and he had rubbed moisturizer into the dry skin between her shoulder blades and trailed his fingers down her spine and toward the small folds of skin above her waist. Julia said, No playing with my love handles. Robert had leaned forward to kiss them and said, Lovely, lovely handles. Robert pulls up a chair and he pats Jewelle on the knee.

"If I may change my mind, coffee would be lovely."

Lionel says, "Maybe some Marion Williams in the background?"

Robert says, "Absolutely. Julia was playing 'Remember Me' just the other day."

The day after the luncheon, they are still cleaning up. Buster washes and Lionel dries and Jewelle, who knows where everything goes, directs the putting away. Patsine sits at the kitchen table, with her feet up on a chair. Buster sings, "Some of these days, you're gonna miss me, honey," and Lionel growls, "Some of these days, you're gonna miss me, babe," and Patsine and Jewelle look at each other, eyes welling up, for their grieving husbands.

"Be useful," Jewelle says to the boys, and she gives them both platters to put into the sideboard. There's no point in giving them the wineglasses. Corinne pokes her head into the kitchen and disappears.

"Corinne," her mother says. "I could use a hand here."

Corinne walks into the middle of the kitchen in her grandmother's black T-shirt, her own yoga pants, her mother's black patent-leather pumps, and a green-and-black silk scarf tied around her neck, Apache-style. ("A-patch," her grandmother said. "It's a dance, not a rodeo.") Her eyes are bright red.

"Nana loved this song," Corinne says. "So, okay."

Buster dries his hands and Lionel and his brother stand with their arms around each other.

"Pretty legs, great big knockers, that's what sells them tickets at the door. Honey, these are real show stoppers, it's what keeps 'em comin' back for more."

Corinne sang this song with her grandmother when no one was home. They shimmied and shook their behinds and one time they both slid down the banister onto pillows. They did the Electric Slide and Nana taught her The Stroll, too, and they danced around the living room like crazy women until they fell onto the couch, laughing and breathless.

"Pretty legs, great big knockers, that's what put the two in two by four. Oooh, baby"—Corinne pauses for her big finish. She struts across the floor like a showgirl and flings open her arms—"Oooh, it ain't the ballads, it ain't the rockers, it's pretty legs and . . . these great . . . big knockers!"

Her father and her uncle whistle and stamp their feet. Ari stares at her, and it's not that sly, slitty look that makes her feel like hiding in the bathroom; his eyes are wide open. Her mother sits down next to Patsine and Patsine is holding Jewelle's hand tightly but they are definitely smiling and Jordan shakes his head in admiration because there is no one like his baby sister. Corinne runs to her mother's lap and buries her head in Jewelle's shoulder. Jewelle puts her arms around her girl and showers her with kisses. Corinne can feel the bump of Patsine's belly pressing behind her and Patsine's hand on her hair.

Robert is standing on the other side of the kitchen, clapping. "Oh, my dear, what a gift," he says. "What a send-off."

Lionel looks at the empty kitchen table and he looks at the clock.

"It's dinner time." He hands food to each person and soon the table is covered with three cartons of Chinese food, from Julia's favorite restaurant, and a deep dish of oyster stuffing and a Tupperware of sweet potatoes with maple syrup and two kinds of chocolate-pecan pie, one for the people who like bourbon and one for people who like it and have to avoid it, and a casserole of creamed spinach with half a nutmeg taped to the top, for the last minute. Jewelle sticks one of the good silver spoons into the bowl of cranberry sauce she brought from home and Buster sets bottles of pear and apple cider and red wine on the table and hands out the crystal wineglasses to everyone. Patsine rests her hands on the baby.

Lionel stands up and lifts his glass and looks at his brother. "Remember this one? A Jewish grandmother and her grandson are playing on the beach, building sandcastles. A wave comes along and drags the poor kid out to sea. The grandmother falls to her knees, screaming and crying. 'Oh, God, oh, God, please save my only grandson. Please, he is the light of my life. Please, God, just save him, that's all I ask of you.' "

"Oh, yeah," Buster says and he stands up. "And another wave comes and drops the little boy back on the beach, good as new. The grandmother hugs and kisses him. Then she looks up at the heavens and says, 'Excuse me? He had a hat.' "

BY-AND-BY

Every death is violent.

The iris, the rainbow of the eye, closes down. The pupil spreads out like black water. It seems natural, if you are there, to push the lid down, to ease the pleated shade over the ball, down to the lower lashes. The light is out, close the door.

Mrs. Warburg called me at midnight. I heard the click of her lighter and the tiny crackle of burning tobacco. Her ring bumped against the receiver.

"Are you comfortable, darling?"

I was pretty comfortable. I was lying on her daughter's bed, with my feet on Anne's yellow quilt, wearing Anne's bathrobe.

"Do you feel like talking tonight?"

Mrs. Warburg was the only person I felt like talking to. My boyfriend was away. My mother was away. My father was dead. I worked in a felafel joint on Charles Street where only my boss spoke English.

I heard Mrs. Warburg swallow. "You have a drink, too. This'll be our little party."

Mrs. Warburg and I had an interstate, telephonic rum-and-

Coke party twice a week the summer Anne was missing. Mrs. Warburg told me about their problems with the house; they had some roof mold and a crack in the foundation, and Mr. Warburg was not handy.

"Roof mold," she said. "When you get married, you move into a nice prewar six in the city and you let some other girl worry about roof mold. You go out dancing."

I know people say, and you see it in movies, cascades of hair tumble out of the coffin, long, curved nails growing over the clasped hands. It's not true. When you're dead, you're dead, and although some cells take longer to die than others, after a few hours everything is gone. The brain cells die fast, and blood pools in the soft, pressed places: the scapula, the lower back, the calves. If the body is not covered up, it produces a smell called cadaverine, and flies pick up the scent from a mile away. First, just one fly, then the rest. They lay fly eggs, and ants come, drawn to the eggs, and sometimes wasps, and always maggots. Beetles and moths, the household kind that eat your sweaters, finish the body; they undress the flesh from the bone. They are the cleanup crew.

Mrs. Warburg and I only talked about Anne in passing and only about Anne in the past. Anne's tenth birthday had had a Hawaiian theme. They made a hot-dog luau in the backyard and served raspberry punch; they played pin-the-lei-on-the-donkey and had grass skirts for all the girls. "Anne might have been a little old for that, even then. She was a sophisticate from birth," Mrs. Warburg said. I was not a sophisticate from birth. I was an idiot from birth, and that is why when the police first came to look for Anne, I said a lot of things that sounded like lies.

Mrs. Warburg loved to entertain; she said Anne was her mother's daughter. We did like to have parties, and Mrs. Warburg made me tell her what kind of hors d'oeuvres we served. She said she was glad we had pigs-in-blankets because that's what she'd served when she was just starting out, although she'd actually made hers. And did one of us actually make the marinara sauce, at least, and was Anne actually eating pork sausage, and she knew it must be me who made pineapple upside-down cake because that was not in her daughter's repertoire, and she hoped we used wine-glasses but she had the strong suspicion we poured wine out of the box into paper cups, which was true. I told her Anne had spray-painted some of our thirdhand furniture bright gold and when we lit the candles and turned out the lights, our apartment looked extremely glamorous.

"Oh, we love glamorous," Mrs. Warburg said.

In the Adirondacks, the Glens Falls trail and the old mining roads sometimes overlap. Miles of trail around Speculator and Johnsburg are as smooth and neatly edged as garden paths. These are the old Fish Hill Mining Company roads, and they will take you firmly and smoothly from the center of Hamilton County to the center of the woods and up the mountainside. Eugene Trask took Anne and her boyfriend, Teddy Ross, when they were loading up Teddy's van in the Glens Falls parking lot. He stabbed Teddy twice in the chest with his hunting knife, and tied him to a tree and stabbed him again, and left him and his backpack right there, next to the wooden sign about NO DRINKING, NO HUNTING. He took Anne with him, in Teddy's car. They found Teddy's body three days later and his parents buried him two days after that, back in Virginia.

Eugene Trask killed another boy just a few days before he killed Teddy. Some kids from Schenectady were celebrating their high school graduation with an overnight camping trip, and when Eugene Trask came upon them, he tied them all to different trees, far enough apart so they couldn't see one another, and then he killed the boy who'd made him mad. While he was stabbing him, the same way he stabbed Teddy, two sharp holes in his heart and then a slash across his chest, for emphasis, for something, the other kids slipped out of their ropes and ran. By the time they came back with people from town, Eugene Trask had circled around the woods and was running through streams, where the dogs could not catch his scent.

The heart is really two hearts and four parts: the right and the left, and the up and the down. The right heart pumps blood through the lungs, the left through the body. Even when there is nothing more for it to do, even when you have already lost ten ounces of blood, which is all an average-size person needs to lose to bring on heart failure, the left heart keeps pumping, bringing old news to nowhere. The right heart sits still as a cave, a thin scrim of blood barely covering its floor. The less air you have, the faster the whole heart beats. Still less and the bronchioles, hollow, spongy flutes of the lungs, whistle and squeeze dry until they lie flat and hard like plates on the table, and when there is no more air and no more blood to bring help from the farthest reaches of the body, the lungs crack and chip like old china.

Mrs. Warburg and I both went to psychics.

She said, "A psychic in East Cleveland. What's that tell you?" which is why I kept talking to her even after Mr. Warburg said he didn't think it was helping. Mrs. Warburg's psychic lived in a run-down split-level ranch house with lime-green shag carpeting. Her psychic wore a white smock and white shoes like a nurse, and she got Mrs. Warburg confused with her three o'clock, who was coming for a reading on her pancreatic cancer. Mrs. Warburg's psychic didn't know where Anne was.

My psychic was on West Cedar Street, in a tiny apartment two blocks away from us on Beacon Hill. My boss's wife had lost a diamond earring and this psychic found it, my boss said. He looked like a graduate student. He was barefoot. He saw me looking down, and flexed his feet.

"Helps me concentrate," he said.

We sat down at a dinette table and he held my hands between his. He inhaled and closed his eyes. I couldn't remember if I had the twenty dollars with me or not.

"Don't worry about it," he said.

We sat for three minutes, and I watched the hands on the grandfather clock behind him. My aunt had the same clock, with cherrywood flowers climbing up the maple box.

"It's very dark," he said. "I'm sorry. It's very dark where she is."

I found the money and he pushed it back at me, and not just out of kindness, I didn't think.

I told Mrs. Warburg my psychic didn't know anything, either.

The police came on Saturday and again on Monday, but not the same ones. On Monday it was detectives from New York, and they did not treat me like the worried roommate. They reminded me that I told the Boston police I'd last seen Anne at two o'clock on Thursday, before she went to Teddy's. They said someone else had told them Anne came back to our apartment at four o'clock, to get her sleeping bag. I said yes, I remembered—I was napping and she woke me up, because it was really my sleeping bag; I lent it to her for the trip. Yes, I did see her at four, not just at two.

Were you upset she was going on this trip with Ted? they said.

Teddy, I said. Why would I be upset?

They looked around our apartment, where I had to walk through Anne's little bedroom to use the bathroom and she had to walk through my little bedroom to get to the front door, as if it were obvious why I'd be upset.

Maybe you didn't like him, they said.

I liked him, I said.

Maybe he was cutting into your time with Annie.

Anne, I said, and they looked at each other as if it was significant that I had corrected them.

Anne, they said. So maybe Teddy got in the way of your friendship with Anne?

I rolled my eyes. No, I said. We double-dated sometimes. It was cool. They looked at their notes.

You have a boyfriend? they said. We'd like to talk to him, too.

Sure, I said. He's in Maine with his family, but you can talk to him.

They shrugged a little. Maine, with parents, was not a promising lead.

They pressed me a little more about my latent lesbian feelings for Anne and my unexpressed and unrequited love for Teddy, and I said that I thought maybe I had forgotten to tell the Boston police that I had worked double shifts every day last week and that I didn't own a car. They smiled and shrugged again.

If you think of anything, they said.

It's very dark where she is, is what I thought.

The police talked to me and they talked to Rose Trask, Eugene's sister, too. She said Eugene was a worthless piece of shit. She said he owed her money and if they found him she'd like it back, please. She hid Eugene's hunting knife at the bottom of her root cellar, under the onions, and she hid Eugene in her big old-fashioned chimney until they left. Later, they made her go up in the helicopter to help them find him, and they made her call out his name over their loudspeaker: "Eugene, I love you. Eugene, it will be okay." While they circled the park, which is three times the size of Yellowstone, she told the police that Eugene had worked on their uncle's farm from the time he was seven, because he was big for his age, and that he knew his way around the woods because their father threw him out of the house naked, in the middle of the night, whenever he wet his bed, which he did all his life.

Mrs. Warburg said she had wanted to be a dancer and she made Anne take jazz and tap and modern all through school but what Anne really loved was talking. Debate Club, Rhetoric, Student Court, Model U.N., anything that gave you plenty of opportunity for arguing and persuading, she liked. I said I knew that because I had had to live with Anne for four years and she had argued and persuaded me out of cheap shoes and generic toilet paper and my mother's winter coat. She'd bought us matching kimonos in Chinatown. I told Mrs. Warburg that it was entirely due to Anne that I was able to walk through the world like a normal person.

Mrs. Warburg said, "Let me get another drink."

I lay back on Anne's bed and sipped my beer. Mrs. Warburg and I had agreed that since I didn't always remember to get rum for our get-togethers, I would make do with beer. Anne actually liked beer, Mrs. Warburg said. Mr. Warburg liked Scotch. Mrs. Warburg went right down the middle, she felt, with the rum and Coke.

"Should we have gone to Teddy's funeral?" she said.

I didn't think so. Mrs. Warburg had never met Teddy, and I certainly didn't want to go. I didn't want to sit with his family, or sit far behind them, hoping that since Teddy was dead, Anne was alive, or that if Anne had to be dead, she'd be lying in a white casket, with bushels of white carnations around her, and Teddy would be lying someplace dark and terrible and unseen.

"I think Anne might have escaped," Mrs. Warburg said. "I really do. I think she might have gotten out of those awful mountains and she might have found a rowboat or something—she's wonderful on water, you should see her on Lake Erie, but it could be because of the trauma she doesn't—"

Mr. Warburg got on the line.

"It's three o'clock in the morning," he said. "Mrs. Warburg needs to sleep. So do you, I'm sure."

Eugene Trask and Anne traveled for four days. He said, at his trial, that she was a wonderful conversationalist. He said that talking to her was a pleasure and that they had had some very lively discussions, which he felt she had enjoyed. At the end of the fourth day, he unbuckled his belt so he could rape her again, in a quiet pine grove near Lake Pleasant, and while he was distracted with his shirttail and zipper, she made a grab for his hunting knife. He hit her on the head with the butt of his rifle, and when she got up, he hit her again. Then he stabbed her twice, just like Teddy, two to the heart. He didn't want to shoot her, he said. He put her bleeding body in the back of an orange Buick he'd stolen in Speculator, and he drove to an abandoned mine. He threw her down the thirty-foot shaft, dumped the Buick in Mineville, and walked through the woods to his sister's place. They had hamburgers and mashed potatoes and sat on Rose's back step and watched a pair of red-tailed hawks circling the spruce. Rose washed out his shirt and pants and ironed them dry, and he left early the next morning, with two meat-loaf sandwiches in his jacket pocket.

They caught Eugene Trask when one of his stolen cars broke down. They shot him in the leg. He said he didn't remember anything since he'd skipped his last arraignment two months ago. He said he was subject to fits of amnesia. He had fancy criminal lawyers who took his case because the hunt for Eugene Trask had turned out to be the biggest manhunt in the tristate area since the Lindbergh baby. There were reporters everywhere, Mrs. Warburg said. Eugene's lawyers, Mr. Feldman and Mr. Barone, told Eugene that if he lied to them they would not be able to defend him adequately, so he drew them maps of where they could find Anne's body, and also two other girls who had been missing for six months. Mr. Feldman and Mr. Barone felt that they could not reveal this information to the police or to the Warburgs or to the other families because it would violate lawyer-client privilege. After the trial, after Eugene was transferred to the Fishkill correctional facility, two kids were playing in an old mine near Speculator, looking for garnets and gold and arrowheads, and they found Anne's body.

The dead body makes its own way. It stiffens and then it relaxes and then it softens. The flesh turns to a black thick cream. If I had put my arms around her to carry her up the gravel path and home, if I had reached out to steady her, my hand would have slid through her skin like a spoon through custard, and she would have fallen away from me, held in only by her clothes. If I had hidden in the timbered walls of the mine, waiting until Eugene Trask heard the reassuring one-two thump of the almost emptied body on the mine-car tracks, I might have seen her as I see her now. Her eyes open and blue, her cheeks pink underneath the streaks of clay and dust, and she is breathing, her chest is rising and falling, too fast and too shallow, like a bird in distress, but rising and falling.

We are all in the cave. Mrs. Warburg went back to her life, without me, after Anne's funeral that winter (did those children find her covered with the first November snow?), and Mr. Warburg resurfaced eight years later, remarried to a woman who became friends with my aunt Rita in Beechwood. Aunt Rita said the new Mrs. Warburg was lovely. She said the first Mrs. Warburg had made herself into a complete invalid, round-the-clock help, but even so she died alone, Rita said, in their old house. She didn't know from what. Eugene Trask was shot and killed trying to escape from Fishkill. Two bullets to the heart, one to the lungs. Mrs. Warburg sent me the clipping. Rose Trask married and had two children, Cheryl and Eugene. Rose and Cheryl and little Eugene drowned in 1986, boating on Lake Champlain. Mrs. Warburg sent me the clipping. My young father, still slim and handsome and a good dancer, collapsed on our roof trying to straighten our ancient TV antenna, and it must have been Eugene Trask pulling his feet out from under him, over the gutters and thirty feet down. Don't let the sun catch you crying, my father used to say. Maybe your nervous system doesn't get the message to swallow the morning toast and Eugene Trask strangles you and throws you to the floor while your wife and children watch. Maybe clusters of secret tumors bloom from skull to spine, opening their petals so Eugene Trask can beat you unconscious on the way to work. Everyone dies of heart failure, Eugene Trask said at his trial.

I don't miss the dead less, I miss them more. I miss the tall pines around Lake Pleasant, I miss the brown-and-gray cobblestones on West Cedar Street, I miss the red-tailed hawks that fly so often in pairs. I miss the cheap red wine in a box and I miss the rum and Coke. I miss Anne's wet gold hair drying as we sat on the fire escape. I miss the hot-dog luau and driving to dance lessons after breakfast at Bruegger's Bagels. I miss the cold mornings on the farm, when the handle of the bucket bit into my small hands and my feet slid over the frozen dew. I miss the hot grease spattering around the felafel balls and the urgent clicking of Hebrew. I miss the new green leaves shaking in the June rain. I miss standing on my father's shiny shoes as we danced to "The Tennessee Waltz" and my mother made me a paper fan so I could flirt like a Southern belle, tapping my nose with the fan. I miss every piece of my dead. Every piece is stacked high like cordwood within me, and my heart, both sides, and all four parts, is their reliquary.

When Your Life Looks Back

When your life looks back—
As it will, at itself, at you—what will it say?

Inch of colored ribbon cut from the spool.
Flame curl, blue-consuming the log it flares from.
Bay leaf. Oak leaf. Cricket. One among many.

Your life will carry you as it did always,
With ten fingers and both palms,
With horizontal ribs and upright spine,
With its filling and emptying heart,
That wanted only your own heart, emptying, filled, in return.
You gave it. What else could do?

Immersed in air or in water.
Immersed in hunger or anger.
Curious even when bored.
Longing even when running away.

"What will happen next?"—
the question hinged in your knees, your ankles,
in the in-breaths even of weeping.
Strongest of magnets, the future impartial drew you in.
Whatever direction you turned toward was face to face.
No back of the world existed,
No unseen corner, no test. No other earth to prepare for.

This, your life had said, its only pronoun.
Here, your life had said, its only house.
Let, your life had said, its only order.

And did you have a choice in this? You did—

Sleeping and waking,
the horses around you, the mountains around you,
The buildings with their tall, hydraulic shafts.
Those of your own kind around you—

A few times, you stood on your head.
A few times, you chose not to be frightened.
A few times, you held another beyond any measure.
A few times, you found yourself held beyond any measure.

Mortal, your life will say,
As if tasting something delicious, as if in envy.
Your immortal life will say this, as it is leaving.

—Jane Hirshfield

WHERE THE GOD OF LOVE HANGS OUT

Farnham is a small town. It has a handful of buildings for the public good and two gas stations and several small businesses, which puzzle everyone (who buys the expensive Italian ceramics, the copper jewelry, the badly made wooden toys?). It has a pizza place and a coffee shop called The Cup.

Ray Watrous looked in The Cup's big window as he walked past. He saw the woman he'd represented in a malpractice suit ten years ago because laminated veneers kept falling out of her mouth. He saw the girl who used to babysit for them when Neil and Jennifer were small, now a fat, homely young woman holding a fat, homely little kid on her lap. He saw his daughter-in-law, Macy, at a table by herself, her gold hair practically falling into her cup, tears running down her face. Ray turned around and went inside. He liked Macy. He was also curious and he was semiretired and he was in no hurry to go to Town Hall and argue with Farnham's first selectman, a decent man suddenly inclined to get in bed with Stop & Shop and put a supermarket in the north end of town, where wild turkeys still gathered.

Ray liked having his son and Macy nearby. Sometimes Ray went down to New Haven for lunch and sometimes Neil drove up to Farnham, on his way to the county courthouse. They talked about sports, and local politics and the collapse of Western civilization. The week before, Neil mentioned that a girl he'd dated in high school was going to run for governor and Ray told Neil that Abe Callender, who shot out the windshield of his own car when he'd found his girlfriend and *her* girlfriend in it, a few years back, was now a state trooper in Farnham.

"Can I join you?" Ray said.

Macy twisted away from him, as if that would keep him from seeing her tears and then she twisted back and took her bag off the other chair.

"Of course," she said.

Randeane, the owner and only waitress of The Cup, brought Ray a black coffee and put down two ginger scones with a dollop of whipped honey on the side.

Ray said, "These scones have Dunkin' Donuts beat all to hell."

Randeane thanked him. "Cream and sugar?"

Ray, who was normally a polite man, said, "The coffee could stand a little fixing up, I guess."

Randeane put her pencil in her pocket and said, "People love our coffee. It's fair trade. Everyone loves our Viennese Roast and our French Roast and I believe people come here *for* our coffee."

Ray said, "I hate to disagree, but they come for the pastries or the atmosphere or because of you but they don't come for the coffee."

"I beg your pardon," Randeane said.

Macy laughed and said, "Wow, Ray."

"I'm just saying, people don't come for the coffee."

"I'll make you a fresh cup."

Randeane brought him another coffee and Ray drank it. It

wasn't great. Macy ate a little bit of her scone and she sighed. Two high school girls sat down at the table next to them.

"I'm not *retarded,*" the skinny girl with pierced eyebrows said.

"I *know.* But, duh, you can't go for a job interview looking like that." The other girl was chubby and cheerful and in a pink uniform.

"Fine," the skinny girl said. "Fix me."

Macy and Ray watched the two girls walk hand in hand into the ladies' room.

"Girls are good at friendship," Ray said.

Macy shrugged. "I guess. I was thinking about my mother when you came in and saw me crying," she said.

"My father was a no-good fall-down drunk," Ray offered. "My mother was as useless as a rubber crutch. But sometimes I miss her. That's the way the dead are, I guess. They come back better than they were."

"We weren't close," Macy said.

She'd been sitting in the kitchen just two days ago, thinking about gumbo and looking for filé powder, when the phone rang. Her mother said hello, she was just passing through and wanted to see Macy. She didn't say *hope to,* or *love to,* she said, "I want to see you, kid. I'm in New Britain. There's a place just off Route 9. It's called the Crab Cake. Meet me there." Her mother wore skinny black jeans and a yellow blouse and high-heeled yellow boots. She had a scarf pulled over her black hair and she sat in a booth, smoking, and when Macy came in, her mother didn't get up.

"Don't you look fat and happy," her mother said.

Macy sat down.

"Surprised?"

"I'm surprised," Macy said. It had been her plan that no one in her real life, meaning Neil and Neil's family, would ever meet her mother.

"I bet. Well, I thought it was time you and your old mother had a chat."

It didn't take very long. Macy called her mother "Betty," which was her given name, and Betty called Macy "Joanie," which was hers. Macy's mother accused Macy of running away and Macy said that if she hadn't run away she'd be a fucked-up coke addict like her mother or worse. Betty said she had done her best and Macy stood up at that point. She said, Don't tell me that. Macy's mother said that they should let bygones be bygones, that she'd dumped Brad's mean, sorry ass anyway, years ago, and see how Joanie had turned out fine. She said she was on her way to Miami and if Joanie could spare her some traveling money, she'd get right into her car. Macy had four hundred dollars she'd put aside from housekeeping money and three hundred she'd gotten as a bonus from her company, another hundred she got for a winter coat she'd returned, and twenty bucks that she'd found in Neil's pants when she took them to the laundry. She'd put it all in an envelope before she got in her car to drive to the Crab Cake and she handed the envelope to her mother, who counted it.

"That's all I have," Macy said. "We're not millionaires."

Her mother was cheerful, the way she always was when things were not as good as she hoped, but not as bad as they could be.

"You weren't hard to find," her mother said.

"I wasn't hiding," Macy said, and her mother smiled and put out her cigarette.

"Well, good. Then you won't mind if I come around again, when I'm passing through."

"You come to my house and I'll shoot you myself. I'll say you snuck in and I shot you in self-defense, thinking you were a burglar. And I will cry my heart out to have killed my own poor, crazy mother, who should have been locked up in the first place."

Macy's mother stood up.

"Aren't you a kidder. It's okay, you lie dormy, and so will I. Good luck," her mother said, and Macy watched her drive off in a dusty blue station wagon.

* * *

A handsome black woman walked past The Cup's big front window.

"Looks like Nellie," Ray said.

"Nellie of the coconut cake," Macy said.

Ray shook his head. "My wife can be a bitch."

Macy said, "I can't argue with you."

Macy and Neil had met at his parents' house. It felt like a houseful of people to Macy, who had lived with one person or none, most of her life. Neil's sister, Jennifer, had brought Macy home with her after they ran into each other their senior year, at the Philadelphia Flower Show. (Just come home with me for the weekend, Jennifer had said. My parents will love you.) Neil was older than Jennifer and Macy by a couple of years and finishing law school; their cousin Howard, who lived in the maid's room because he couldn't face the real world after his time in Afghanistan, was making drinks for everyone.

Jennifer said, "This is Macy. You'll love her."

Neil squeezed Macy's hand and looked her right in the eye and she could feel herself blushing. Eleanor Watrous served chicken fricassee with dumplings and glazed carrots and a separate plate of bitter green salad with a disk of goat cheese in the middle. For dessert, Jennifer carried in a gigantic and snowy and objectively beautiful coconut cake.

Macy said, "My goodness, that's gorgeous."

Mrs. Watrous waved her hand toward the kitchen and said that Nellie was gifted. (That's the housekeeper, Neil said quietly. She cooks when my mother wants to impress people.) "I'll have Nellie wrap some up for you," Mrs. Watrous said, so that everyone could just picture Macy in her windowless room, sitting on her twin bed, unwrapping the slice of cake for a snack or for breakfast. Macy let her napkin slide to the floor so she could get a grip on herself.

Neil's hand came crab-walking across the rug, toward Macy's napkin. He stroked her ankle and then he picked up the napkin and put it in her lap.

After coffee, Mr. Watrous had said, Let's adjourn and Neil and Cousin Howard followed him into the study. The door to the study was not closed, and Macy sat in the chair nearest the door.

"Cute girl, Jennifer's little friend," Neil's father said.

"She's hot," Cousin Howard said, and then he picked up a magazine and started fanning himself.

"Christ, Howard," Mr. Watrous said. "How's law school, Neil?"

"Okay," Neil said.

"Getting any offers?"

"A few."

"Stay out of the pigpen," Mr. Watrous said.

Cousin Howard said, "Soo-eee. Here, piggy, piggy, piggy," and Mr. Watrous said, "For the love of Jesus," and the men came back into the living room. Neil sat down on the arm of Macy's chair and patted her hair.

Sunday afternoon, he drove Macy and Jennifer to the train station. He told his sister to go get the tickets and behind her, he kissed Macy, his narrow lips opening like a flower. He smelled of cinnamon and smoke.

The next time Macy and Neil visited the Watrouses, they were a couple.

Mrs. Watrous asked Macy to help set the table, just to see if she knew where the glasses went and in what order. Macy laid glasses down over knives, water, white, and red, exactly as Emily Post recommended, and Neil's mother glanced over and said, as if it wasn't a test at all, Oh, who cares, really? These days, you could put a jug and four bowls on the table, couldn't you? Let's move to the patio. Macy drank three glasses of water, she was so nervous, and after Neil's father had asked about her parents and Macy had said that they were dead and that her only relatives were an aunt and uncle in Des Moines, they moved on to Macy's favorite classes. Everything went pretty well until Macy took a green olive out of the bowl next to her. It stuck to the roof of her mouth, its tip digging into the soft part at the back. She choked until she spat out the jalapeño pepper the olive was stuffed with, crying and swearing, Goddammit, oh, mother*fucker,* and Neil jumped up to get her water. Mr. Watrous said those olives were going to kill someone and Mrs. Watrous said that he'd eaten about fifteen of them so far. Finally, Macy took the glass of water from Neil and, in her relief, relaxed her arm and pushed the olive bowl onto the stone floor. Mrs. Watrous walked to the kitchen for a thick dishcloth and Nellie the cook came in behind her with a dustpan and the glass shards were disappeared. When Mrs. Watrous came back, Macy said, My God, I am *so* sorry. And Mrs. Watrous said, It's all right. If I were the Queen of England, I'd have to throw another Baccarat bowl on the floor, just to make you feel at ease.

Macy was silent for the rest of dinner.

That's what I get, she thought. You listen and you listen and you copy their ways and who fucking knew that that bat, that blond bat in a Lilly Pulitzer sheath with her fucking family retainers, who knew I'd break her fucking Baccarat. Macy lived in a boardinghouse a mile from campus and cleaned all the rooms in the house on Saturdays for a break on her rent. On weekends she went to parties and had people drop her off at a trolley stop. She didn't have people over. She didn't go on vacation with other people's families. The girls Macy hung around with, girls like Jennifer and her friends, thought Macy lived with rich, strict relatives. They'd never seen a boardinghouse or a carpet sweeper or a shared bathroom. They didn't make their meals on a hot plate in their room, unless they were doing it for fun, and they didn't read Emily Post and Miss Manners like the Old and the New Testament.

Macy brought her lunch to campus every day and she ate in the handicapped-access bathroom. Afterward, she sat in the Student Center to socialize, and when the other girls ate two slices of whole-wheat pizza or a big bowl of soba noodles or a roast-beef sandwich, Macy smiled like Pietsie Cortland, who also didn't eat, for more normal reasons. Pietsie was Macy's favorite. Macy loved everything about Pietsie, including her name, which was so fancy, Macy wanted to take her aside and say, Good for you. (When they did get into the question of background, Pietsie said, Isn't it awful—it's for Van Piet, my middle name. You know, old name, *no* money, not a pot to piss in, and Macy heard the *ping* of real crystal.) Macy avoided anyone who seemed remotely interested in her family. Interesting was not good.

"It's okay," Neil had said on the way back to his apartment. "My mother has a strong personality. It'll be okay."

Macy looked down at her hands, twisting in her lap.

"It'll be okay," Neil said, "because I love you. Ha," he said, when she stared at him. "You didn't know that, did you?"

"No," Macy said, and she put her head on his shoulder and cried a little, at the thought of being loved by Neil Watrous, who was apparently without serious fault.

Neil pulled over and they kissed and then they drove to his apartment. They ran up the stairs, and by the time Neil had unlocked the door, Macy had her shoes and her blouse off and she flung herself on top of him, kissing his floppy brown hair and his big ears and the nicks where he'd cut himself shaving. They landed on his sofa. He kissed her stomach and her armpits. He ran his tongue from her ankle to her ear and they bit each other at every round and yielding spot. At one point, they found themselves with their heads hanging off the bed, their bare feet making dark, damp prints all the way up his wall.

"I was made to love you," Neil said. He sang the whole Stevie Wonder song, naked, with his head touching the floor.

"And I you," Macy said.

* * *

The summer before she'd met Neil, even though she was pretty sure that what she was looking for was not creative expression but something more like the makeover to end all makeovers, Macy had spent a week on scholarship at a writers' conference. She looked at the men and women around her and thought, We're like the people at Lourdes or the ones who go to the mud baths of that disgusting town with the sulfurous pools that everyone dunks themselves in, except we've brought our poems and short stories and inexpressible wishes, instead of scrofula and dermatitis.

She smoked like a chimney and wrote about whatever came into her head, but only for a few pages and then she ran out of steam. She wrote about the man who sat next to her in the workshop, a seventy-five-year-old engineer from Salt Lake City, trying desperately to come out of the closet after sixty years and a wife, two kids, and six grandchildren. The engineer invited Macy out for a drink after class and they found a small table at a bad restaurant. He put his hand on Macy's and said, Dear, I love men. I know, Macy said. Everyone in their workshop knew; the engineer wrote about thighs like steel girders and asses like ball bearings and biceps like pistons. It's fine, Macy said. I love them, too. The engineer said, Women, I mean their private parts, make me want to vomit. Present company excepted, of course. Well, then you're making the right choice, Macy said. She swallowed her vodka gimlet and went to another reading. She went to every reading and performance that was scheduled and she went late, in hopes of finding a seat next to a good-looking man, or even just a nice man, and she stood in line to have books signed by people she thought were complete idiots, just to improve the odds. She wrote down a few other things that happened at the writers' conference, in a lavender suede notebook, and then she threw the notebook into the dumpster.

The day after he and Macy had had their tête-à-tête in the coffee shop, Ray stopped in on his way home.

"I hope I'm not keeping you," Ray said.

Randeane smiled and said he wasn't and she poured his coffee.

"Randeane," Ray said. "That's sort of a Southern name, isn't it?"

"Left-wing Jewish father, hence the Jewfro"—she ran her fingers through her curly hair—"and white-trash Pentecostal mother, hence the Randeane and the inability to finish my thesis. Yourself?"

Ray said that his parents weren't that interesting. English peddlers on his father's side, Norwegian farmers on his mother's, and really not much to them.

"Well, take some scones home. I'll just have to toss them tomorrow and I will be goddamned fuck-fried if I'm going to stay up and make bread pudding all night."

"Absolutely not. Someone must be waiting up for you," Ray said, and he thought that although it was difficult to imagine dying of embarrassment at his age, it wasn't impossible.

"Not really," Randeane said, and she handed him a shopping bag of scones.

Neil had come to Ray a few weeks after the coconut cake dinner and told his father that he planned to ask Macy to marry him. Ray meant to say, Congratulations, but he heard himself say that although people of his generation married for life, he, personally, thought it was one of the worst and stupidest ideas ever foisted on mankind, second only to Jesus died for our sins, which was just ridiculous. Neil looked at him, a little cow-eyed, and Ray meant to shut up but instead he said, Everyone who gets divorced feels betrayed, whichever side you're on. But what's worse—everyone who gets married feels betrayed. The other person will let you down, son—they can't help it. We are all basically selfish beasts, and also, your wife will love your children more than she will ever love you. You're just the hod carrier, kid. You know what your mother says: You promised to love me for better or worse, Ray Watrous.

Neil said, "I understand, Dad. I mean, I do." He put his hand on Ray's shoulder and Ray was sorry he'd opened his mouth. "It's a little different for me and Macy. It's just different for us."

"I'm sure it is," Ray said. "She's a lovely girl. Let's not keep our brides waiting."

A lot of Ray's friends called their wives their brides. Ray referred to Ellie that way once, in The Cup, saying, "I'll bring some of these bagels home to my bride," and Randeane flinched.

"That's an awful expression," she said. "It's like you keep her in a closet with a white dress and veil. Your very own Miss Havisham."

"Not at all," Ray said. "It shows I still think of her the way I did when we were first married. It's flattering."

"In a pig's eye," Randeane said, and she shoved the bagels in a bag and threw Ray's change on the counter.

Before winter started, Ray bought a dog. ("Do you even like dogs?" Eleanor said.) He walked it every night past Randeane's house. Often Randeane was reading on her front porch; sometimes she was around the back, where she had a hammock, an outdoor fireplace, and two white plastic lounge chairs.

"Hammock or chaise longue?" Randeane said.

Ray said that he was more a chair kind of person, that hammocks were unpredictable.

"Oh, life's a hammock," Randeane said.

"Exactly my point. I'll take the chair."

"Remember Oscar? You met him once. He's asked me to marry him," Randeane said.

Ray sighed.

"Don't sigh," she said.

"That's what Ellie says to me. She says, 'Don't sigh, Ray, this is not the Gulag.' You know what else she says—after a few drinks, she says, 'Ray, I promised to love you for better or worse.' No one should make such a promise. I don't think I even know what it means—for better or for worse. Why would you be married to someone for worse?"

"You don't think I should marry him?"

"I met him once," Ray said. "Firm handshake."

"Come lie in the hammock."

"I can't do that," Ray said.

"I'm pretty sure you can," Randeane said. She kicked off her green slippers and climbed into the hammock. Her pants pulled up to her calves. "At least you can push me." Ray gave her a push and sat down again.

"You could marry me," Ray said. "We both know I'd be a better choice."

Randeane looked up at the sky. "I guess so," she said. "You, younger, single, maybe not so deeply pissed off and inflexible."

"I don't think we'll be seeing that," Ray said, and he stumbled a little getting off the chaise and took the dog home. He drove to The Yankee Clipper for a beer.

The parking lot was barely half full and Ray knew most of the cars. Leo Ferrante's BMW, that would be Leo, celebrating having persuaded the people in charge of Farnham that neither a Stop & Shop nor a horse crematorium was anything to get upset about. Leo would be drinking with his clients and sitting near Anne Fishbach. Every Tuesday night, Anne left her senile husband with a nurse and drove over to the Clipper. ("Aren't I allowed?" she'd said to Ray. "Does this make me a bad wife? After fifty-three years?") She sat in a back booth and drank Manhattans until someone drove her home.

Ray recognized his next-door neighbor's green pickup. He

saw two guys from the Exchange Club walk out of the bar and recognize *his* car and Ray knew enough to go somewhere else. He drove about ten miles and pulled into a town he'd been to only once, twenty years ago, to pick up Jennifer from a Girl Scout jamboree. There were two bars, on either side of the wide main street. One awning said PADDY O'TOOLE'S BAR AND GRILLE and had gold four-leaf clovers in the window and on the awning. The other said BUCK'S SAFARI BAR and had a poster of Obama in one window and in the other, a poster of a black girl, with an enormous cloud of black curls, standing with her oiled legs apart, falling out of a tiny leopard-skin bikini. Ray thought, When it's your time, it's your time, and he went in.

No one minded him. Back in the day, some young man might have felt compelled to defend his manhood or his blackness or the virtue of a waitress and Ray might have found himself scuffling on a wet wood floor or a hard sidewalk, but not now. A young woman and her date slid off their barstools into a booth and the man indicated that Ray was free to take the man's seat. The barmaid was short and wide, wearing a gold leather skirt and gold nail polish. Her hair was cut close to the scalp and dyed blond. She put a napkin in front of Ray and looked at him the way she looked at every other man at the bar.

"Just a beer, please. Whatever's on tap."

He could stay in Buck's all night. He could probably move into Buck's. They seemed like nice people. They were certainly a lot more tolerant of an old white man in their midst than the people at the Clipper would be if some strange black guy bellied up to the bar. Ray ordered another beer and a burger and he watched the Steelers crush the Colts.

"Christ," Ray said, "no defense at all."

"I hear you," the man next to him said, and someone tapped Ray on the shoulder.

Ray's elbow tipped his glass and the man to his left caught it and the barmaid said, Good catch, and Macy was standing beside him.

"What in Christ's name are you doing here?" Ray said. "Where's Neil?" In the five years since the wedding, Ray had never seen Macy take a drink, let alone in a black bar at the ass end of Meriden.

Macy shrugged. "I used to live around here," she said. "I took a drive and . . . You want to get a booth?"

"I would," said the man on Ray's left. "I would definitely get a booth."

"She's my daughter-in-law," Ray said.

"Let he who is without sin, cast the first stone," the man said.

"I thought you were from Iowa. Kansas? Was I wrong?" Ray said, when they'd brought their beers to a table.

"No. I said my parents were dead and I had an aunt and uncle in Des Moines. Which I don't."

Macy drummed her fingers on the table.

"I love Neil," she said. "I really do."

"I'm sure you do. And he loves you. Christ, you have only to look at him—he thinks you hung the moon."

"Really? He wants to have a baby."

"Good," Ray said. "Have two." Babies having babies, he thought.

"He thinks I hung the moon? He's the best man I know," Macy said. "I'm just not who he thinks I am."

"That's not the worst thing in the world," Ray said, and Macy put her hand, cool and wet from the beer, over his lips. Her hand smelled like grapefruit.

"I don't mean he doesn't know my essence on some metaphysical level. I mean I have lied to him on a million different occasions about a million things."

Ray nodded.

"When I was ten, my mother fell down on the kitchen floor,

and blood was pouring out of her nose. So, you know, I understood she was OD'ing on coke."

Ray nodded again, like women OD'ing on coke in front of their children was as much part of his life as reading the paper.

"I had this amazing babysitter, Sammy. So—I don't want this to take forever—when I'm fourteen my mother moves in with this guy, we'll just call him The Asshole, and I moved in with Sammy. It turns out, Sammy's a transvestite."

Ray nodded again; he had defended a dozen middle-aged guys in dresses who were caught speeding.

"So, I do Sammy's hair and nails. And I do his friends', too, and Sammy basically sets me up in the tranny business in our TV room. I do hair, nails, and makeup every day after school and most of Saturday. When I graduate from high school, I have three thousand dollars in my savings account. Plus, I got into Bryn Mawr on scholarship *and* I graduated second in my class." Macy smiled shyly. "My name's not Macy. I changed it—I mean I changed it legally, when I was sixteen. Sammy's mother's name was Macy. So when we get to Bryn Mawr, Sammy is just the *shit*. All the parents *love* him. He drives off and he goes, *Au revoir,* honeybun, and don't look back. He got a horrible staph infection, from the acrylic nails. Ten days in the ICU. It was terrible. He was a really, really nice man," Macy said, wiping her face with a beer napkin.

"When I was in college," Ray said, "I let a guy give me a blow job. Let me be clear. This guy paid me fifty bucks, which was a lot of money at the time, and I let him do me once a week for three years. If not for him, I would have had to drop out of college. You already know my father was a bum."

"Thank you," Macy said, and she laughed. Ray smiled.

"Also, you might already know this—I'm in love with Randeane."

"I really like her," Macy said. "Everything about her, she's just so great. She's read everything. *I'm* sort of in love with her."

"Maybe," Ray said. He sighed and spread his arms along the back of the booth. "I'm pretty sure not like this."

One morning, Ray told Macy, he'd gotten to Randeane's late, between the morning people and the lunchtime people, and there was a man sitting at Ray's usual table.

Oh, Ray, Randeane said. This is my friend, Garbly Garble. Ray couldn't make out the man's name. He was taller than Ray, in his late thirties or early forties; it was harder and harder for Ray to tell anything except that someone was more or less his age. People under fifty looked like young people and people under thirty looked like children. The man stood up politely and shook Ray's hand. He shook it twice, not the hard handshake that even men Ray's age gave one another just to show they were still in the game, but a very gentle, slow handshake as if he was mindful of Ray's osteoporosis or arthritis or some other damned thing that would make Ray's hand crumble in his like an Egyptian relic. The man was clearly not thinking, So, this is the competition; he was thinking, Poor old Uncle Ray, or even poor Grandpa Ray, Civil War veteran. Nurse, get this man a chair. Ray walked out and across town to the office of Ferrante and Ticknor, Attorneys-at-Law. He walked along the narrow, cluttered river that ran through the park.

In Leo Ferrante's office, Ray cleared his throat and Leo put his hand up.

"Don't," he said.

"What, you're psychic?" Ray said.

Leo said he was sorry, that in the past three days he'd had two old friends come in to divorce their wives and marry hot chicks.

"I wouldn't call her a hot chick," Ray'd said.

Macy leaned forward, her face in her hands, lit up with the thought of Ray's love for Randeane. She looked about twelve years old.

"You deserve happiness, Ray."

"And Eleanor? What about her happiness?"

Macy did not say that Eleanor's happiness was of no account to her.

Ray said, "Someone's got to speak up for Ellie," and he looked around Buck's as if the gold-haired bartender or the young couple might say something on Ellie's behalf. Like: Goddammit, that woman has—in her own way—devoted herself to you. Or maybe the bartender would say, Leave Ellie and your children will turn their backs on you. They think you're a good man. Leave Ellie to shack up with a young lady from the coffee shop, half your age. No fool like an old fool. Ray turned back to Macy but he could still hear the bartender and Leo Ferrante talking to him. Your prostate alone's enough to scare her off; you gotta get a guest room just to keep it somewhere. And your suitcase of Viagra and Levitra and don't forget the Allopurinol and the Amlodipine and the Flomax, without which you'll never piss again. And why shouldn't she want children, young as she is? She could have them with that tall, good-looking man, Ray heard the bartender say, and he looked at her and she winked, gold powder sparkling on her eyelids and cheekbones, shining across her breasts. She brought them another pair of beers and a bowl of nuts.

"Do you have any food?" Macy said.

"What do you like?" the woman said.

Macy looked around and she sniffed the air.

"Catfish, maybe," she said.

The woman shrugged pleasantly. "For two? Sweet-potato fries? Butter beans?"

"I have died and gone to heaven," Macy said, and she almost clapped her hands.

"I don't think I can eat all that," Ray said.

"I love it. I'll bring some home for Neil. Like they say, so good, makes you want to slap yo' mama." Macy took a sip of beer and smiled. "Sammy was a great cook. Actually, I'm a great cook."

Turned on a dime, Ray thought. Two hours ago, she was going to hang herself in the garage because Neil didn't know her essence;

now she's bringing him a Southern fried feast and they'll eat in bed. Laughing. Ray thought of Randeane and his heart clenched so deeply, he put his hands on the table.

"You *should* bring some home for him. I really can't eat that stuff anymore," he said. "Call him. Tell him you're coming home. Don't be afraid to tell him about your mother and about Sammy. He'll admire you for that stuff. For getting past it."

"Okay," Macy said, biting her lip. "You really think so?" She took out her phone and checked her text messages.

"He's still at work," she said, grinning like a kid. "He's not even worrying." She texted Neil and showed Ray: *B home soon, w fab dinner. Love u so.*

A big man came out of the kitchen and laid their food in front of them. He nodded toward the game on TV.

"That game's over," he said. "You know what Archie Griffin said, 'Ain't the size of the dog in the fight but the size of the fight in the dog.' These guys got no fight."

"Hell of a player, Griffin. Two Heismans."

The man paused, like he might sit down, and Macy moved over to make room.

"Great tailback," the man said.

"Well, they measure these things differently now," Ray said. "For my money, Bronko Nagurski was the greatest running back."

"Ah," the man said. "Played both sides of the ball. You don't see that anymore."

"No you don't," Ray said.

The man slipped the bill under Ray's plate. "Come back soon."

"Ray," Macy said. "If you want to be with Randeane, if you need, I don't know, support, I'll be there for you. Neil, too."

Ray picked at the fries, which were the best fries he could remember eating. If he did nothing else to improve his life, he could come to Buck's every few weeks, have a beer and a plate of sweet-potato fries, and talk football with the cook.

Macy tapped the back of his hand with her fork. "Ray. You be the quarterback and I'll be, I'll be the guy who protects the quarterback. I'll be that guy."

"Honey," Ray said. "There's really no one like that in football."

Right after Jennifer was born, they found cyst after cyst inside of Ellie, and when Jennifer was two, Ellie had a hysterectomy. Ray brought her an armful of red stargazer lilies from the florist, not from the grocery store or the hospital gift shop, because Ellie was particular about things like that, and when he walked in, she smiled, closed her compact, and set her lipstick on the bedside table. She'd brought her blue silk bathrobe from home and had brushed her hair back in a ponytail and tied it with a blue ribbon. She made room for Ray on the bed and they held hands.

"The kids are fine," Ray said. "Nellie's got Neil making the beds and Jennifer's running into the wall about ten times a day. Then she falls down and laughs like a lunatic."

"Oh, good," Ellie said, and she looked out the window and sighed.

"Hey, no sighing," Ray said. "Everything's all right."

Ellie said, "No, it's not. I wanted one more baby. I wanted to be like everyone else. I didn't want to go into menopause at thirty-three, thank you very much, and I am not looking forward to having Dr. Perlmutter's hand up my you-know-what every six months for the rest of my life."

Ray squeezed her hand. "For better or for worse. Isn't that what we said? So, this is a little bit of worse."

Ellie tossed his hand aside and squinted at him, like the sexy, fearless WACs he admired when he was a boy, girls who outran and outgunned the guys, even in skirts and heels.

"You think this is worse?" Ellie said. "Oh, shame on me. Sweetie, if this is what worse looks like—we'll be just fine."

She'd said the same thing when his blood pressure medication chased away his erections and Viagra brought them back, but not the same. They were unmistakably old-man erections; they were like old men themselves: frail and distracted and unsure. He'd lain in bed with his back to her, ashamed and sorry for himself. Ellie turned on the light to look at him. She had her pink silk nightgown on and her face was shiny with moisturizer. She pulled up on one elbow and leaned around him. He saw the creases at her neck and between her breasts, the tiny pleats at her underarms, the little pillow of flesh under her sharp chin, and he thought, She must be seeing the same thing. She snapped off the light and put her hand on his shoulder.

"So what, Ray? You think this is the worst? You think, finally, we've gotten to 'for worse'?"

Maybe not for you, Ray thought.

"It's not. It's not better, but it's not the worse," she said.

Eleanor slid her hand under the covers and wrapped her fingers around his cock. She gave a little squeeze, like a salute. She pushed the covers back and pressed him onto his back. She talked while she stroked him. She told him about the guy who had come to do the patio and brought his four giant dogs with him; she told him about seeing one of Neil's friends from high school who'd said, when she asked how his mother was, Great, she's out on parole; she told him that she'd heard that young men shaved their balls now. Ray lifted his head and asked her if she would like that. I guess I would, she said. Is it unpleasant otherwise? Ray said. Oh, I don't know, Ellie said. It's like a mouthful of wet mitten—what do *you* think? When he stopped laughing, early in the morning, with a faint light falling on Ellie's silver hair held back with a pink ribbon and her slim, manicured hands, he came.

* * *

Ray followed Macy home from Buck's. He could see her dark outline in the car when they drove under a streetlight, her right arm up the whole time, talking on her phone. She honked twice when she got to her driveway and pulled in. Their porch light snapped on and the moths gathered. Macy ran onto the porch and Ray could see Neil, in just his underwear, reaching out for her with both arms.

Ray turned left instead of right and parked in front of Randeane's. From the car, he saw the white edge of her chaise. He saw just the green tips of her slippered feet. He honked twice and drove home.

ACKNOWLEDGMENTS

My editor, Kate Medina, continues to be not only my brave and erudite captain but a dear friend and wise counselor. My agent, Phyllis Wender, continues to be the standard by which literary agents should be measured; her warm intelligence and steadfastness are legendary.

I am grateful to both the MacDowell Colony and the Yaddo Foundation, as more than a few of these stories were written in those places.

I am blessed with my beloved family of readers, Alexander, Caitlin, and Sarah, all exceptionally literate, all straight talkers, all my favorite people. I am grateful to my friends Kay Ariel and Bob Bledsoe, as well, for their generous criticism and sturdy support and for much more than that. Richard McCann has continued to be my eleventh-hour hero, with timely, stringent, and compassionate criticism. I have also been immeasurably assisted by Jennifer Ferri, who has made my business hers, in the best possible way.

ABOUT THE TYPE

This book was set in Bembo, a typeface based on an old-style Roman face that was used for Cardinal Bembo's tract *De Aetna* in 1495. Bembo was cut by Francisco Griffo in the early sixteenth century. The Lanston Monotype Company of Philadelphia brought the well-proportioned letterforms of Bembo to the United States in the 1930s.